# The Losing
# of These
# Things

# Kelly Jurgensen

B&H Bennett &
Hastings Publishing

Bennett & Hastings titles may be ordered through booksellers or by contacting: sales@ bennetthastings.com or writing to 2400 NW 80th Street #254, Seattle WA 98117


Editor: Adam Finley

Cover art by: Marty Rogers


ISBN: 978-1-934733-63-9 paperback

# THE LOSING OF THESE THINGS

For my Leslie
We've been thru
a lot of horses
together!
Always—
H.J.

*"This one's for you, Mom!"*

# CONTENTS

# BELLYDANCING

Like it or not, certain men stand out in a woman's life and three stand out in mine: my father; the man I married; and Luke O'Connor.

I often thought Dad was chosen by the universe to teach me patience. He said he'd thought the very same thing of me. When I decided to go to graduate school and explore my Celtic roots by studying Druid Philosophy, Dad was the first person I told – which turned out to be a mistake.

"Druid Philosophy? You're pulling my leg, right?"

Reminding myself how Dad had always wanted me to go on with my drama studies, play his little girl forever, I smiled with exaggerated patience.

"No, I'm not pulling your leg, but I would be if I were to think I had a future on the stage, Dad."

Dad's strategy was similar to my own. He exercised tolerance and humor at will. "Ok, darling. I think I see it now. Just took me a moment, that's all. Druid Philosophy, eh?"

I nodded cautiously.

"So what're you going to do with it – become a Druid?"

I waited, stone-faced, until he quit laughing. "It's not funny, Dad. I'm serious."

"Hell, I know you're serious, that's what makes it so damn funny. Why don't you take up belly dancing while you're at it? It'd probably pay more. Ah, heck … go on, go ahead and ride the horse in the direction it's going, my Celtic cowgirl, I can't stop you."

It was the closest I ever came to an actual blessing from Dad.

---

The first words Matthew Mason spoke to me were these: "If God were a woman, I'd imagine her to look just like you. Hello. My name is Matthew Mason and I'm instructing this class."

I should have heard those words for the projection that they were – the mantra of a lonely man in need of a woman big as God – and run like hell, but I didn't.

Instead I looked up from placing my books on a desk in the front row. As usual I was the first one into the classroom, an old habit forced on me by my mother at an early age. It was a habit I clung to through high school when my height and size kept me from winning any popularity contests – I never was one to mingle with classmates in the hall.

Frankly, I was lonely too, but his remarks caught me so by surprise I didn't know whether to shake his outstretched hand or to laugh and shrug the whole thing off. I was also flattered, and wondered what quick return I was capable of to keep his interest forthcoming. No words came though, so straightening up from a stooped position over the desk I took a deep breath and felt my body rise to its full height of six foot two and a half.

The sudden silence that rose between us then was anything but a bridge. My size often had this effect on men and usually they withdrew. But Mat didn't seem to notice the silence which should have served as a warning to us both, and instead kept gazing at me like a rock climber who has found the perfect peak to scale.

"Ssssh … I don't want to know your name yet. I prefer to think of you as Artemus. A-ha, Artemus who has left her wild animal friends and the forest to mingle with the common people."

I couldn't have resisted if I'd wanted to. Here was a man who had me pegged for an archetype: a woods nymph, a goddess even. Who was I to tell him he was wrong?

---

I suppose I fell in love with Mat because he seemed older, and because he seemed wiser. He was older, but not necessarily wiser. It was just one more illusion of mine put to rest, made sober by years of observation – if not downright participation.

The first time I brought him home to my parents, I heard my mother say the words of prayerful thanks she would voice whenever something she'd only allowed herself to dream about came forward as fact. My husband to be came forward as fact, extending his hand quickly, his eyes searching hers as he assessed the large personality he had only heard stories about, encased in the tiny figure who was my mother. "Praise be the Lord," she whispered once, and seemed about to whisper again, until she caught my eye peering over Matthew's shoulder. It wasn't that Mom ever meant to embarrass me. She just did. Especially when it came to prayers of thanks or forgiveness for events which took place in her grown children's lives that seemed to effect her more than they did us.

"A-ha, Mrs. Lee, what a pretty lady you are."

I quietly let go of the breath I'd been holding and agreed, as if she were my daughter instead of me hers.

Matthew beamed at her and patted the delicate hand she enclosed in his as if beating a small drum. As they stood there inches apart, sending sunshine into one another's faces, I had a sense of not belonging, an uneasy feeling born of a brooding isolation on the one hand and too much time spent with dogs and horses on the other.

"You must stay for dinner," said my mother. I shuffled forward, hoping to capture her attention before it ran off with Matthew, who was already inspecting the small living room that immediately invited anyone entering the front door, to go on and enter it next. I mouthed a big No and turned my palms towards the sky, along with the head tilt which Mom always referred to as my infamous 'Ah gee, Ma' look. But it was too late. Matthew's bright countenance agreed with the invitation. He finished his tour of the living room and started into the small kitchen that served as the dining room. Mom trotted after him, but stopped so quickly I nearly tripped on her heels.

"Becky, he's wonderful," she whispered. "Where on earth did you find him? Praise, oh praise be and silly me, I know where you found him. I always knew you'd do well in college, dear." And with a giggle, she followed Matthew, her bedroom slippers slap-slapping an echo in the hall. Rolling my eyes, I trudged after her, consoling myself with the reminder that Mom was displaying the ecstasy of two parents, now that Dad was dead.

—·—

So Mat and I were married. M&M was what I called him: his initials, my favorite candy. He called me his Almond Joy because I was his favorite nut covered in light chocolate, the latter a reference aimed at the deep tan I cultivated each summer by taking out trail rides for a nearby dude ranch – a job I managed to pry myself away from after we were married. The fact that Mat wasn't the first man I gave up horses for was beside the point. Or maybe it was the point, one I failed to see until it was almost too late.

Everyone except my mother called us things they didn't dare say to our faces, but I didn't care. If nothing else, I was sure they'd come to love me as his partner in life, and so I warded off the verbal low shots and rumors which came in the form of mean spirited quips about our differences in family backgrounds.

There were differences. But I considered them Matthew's loss, not mine. So what if his father was deemed important enough to run after votes for governor? My father used to run after bulls as a rodeo clown when he got too old to cowboy himself. Besides, having been raised by a matriarch, I was more impressed by queens than governors. What's more, I had a small town faith in the sanctity of ritual, that of marriage, specifically.

But after we were married it didn't seem to change the sentiment one iota, and well beyond the surge and ebb of being newlyweds, I managed to wield a personal power simply by virtue of a small town's need to have its very own witch and fallen woman. The only place I'd ever fallen from to my knowledge was a horse, and I'd always thought of witches as capable of casting spells. I couldn't even cast a proper line into the water when fishing with my husband, nor could I cast aside his belief that I needed to either.

But it was useless to point such facts out. Small towns seemed to have a need for tall tales. And the fact is I'd always liked playing major roles, especially in a town where boredom had become a step up from apathy. I mean, why confine the art of drama to a mere wooden platform anyway? So I continued to play the part of a clever crook whose naive husband would eventually see the error of his ways and trade his wife for a more complementary woman, someone who would smile graciously and stick like a shadow by his side at collegiate cocktail parties and academic functions.

And they were right. I would never be the feminine counterpart of Matthew Mason. I was born the eldest of four children, and had always been expected to carry my own weight. I was six foot two and a half, and had carried several pounds more than I needed through most of my adolescence, the memory of which still haunts me.

Today I wear faded Levis with the best of them, and I suppose my tee shirts, complete with words suggesting the politics I'm too apologetic to state out loud, will always fit too snugly. And when I top it all off with one of the many western-styled hats I can't help but collect, I guess I look more like the Malboro Man than Cindy Crawford. But what the heck, as Dad always said.

Although I've been told all my life that I'm a big girl, I've come to understand the dual meaning and intent that's held by small women and all sizes of men by that line. I do have a large frame, thus I'm capable of carrying more weight. But back before I was even ten years old, I was also the big girl who was not to cry when she fell, or feel hurt by some small fry of a mean kid's cruel words.

And when my father died, I was the one who lifted my tiny mother up into my arms where her heart could beat its pain against my own. So it could have been said I carried my own weight, but it could have been said I carried more than my share, too.

Which isn't to make light of the fact that I did take a seat in the easy chair of acquiescence once too often, leaving most decisions, and even my own choices, up to Mat. But all that changed one summer when our boat got stuck in a bank of the Saint John's River on an outgoing tide.

———

We'd bought the boat after a particularly tough spring semester had ended for Mat. The boat helped him see that there was light at the end of the tunnel and it wasn't a head on collision either. The summer before he had taught me to fish, so the addition of a boat was both practical and romantic. I had no experience with either boats or long trips on bodies of water, and though I was uneasy at first, Mat's self-confidence was reassuring.

Several days after purchasing the boat, but only a few days after the beginning of summer had worn off (along with Mat's teacher's tension), he set his mug of tea down on the kitchen counter at breakfast and announced, "Let's do it, let's take that trip!"

Initially I thought he meant the trip we'd always talked about, the trip to his grandfather's cabin in Maine – his grandfather was dead but the cabin was open to any relatives who wished to use it. I'd been wishing to use it from the day I learned it existed, and since I was still tense from Mat's teaching, the idea began percolating in my mind like a fresh cup of coffee. It was a perfect suggestion too: Mat could fish and think to his mind's content and I could roam the woods and the lakeside, write poetry, or long overdue letters. I cupped my hands around my mug of steaming tea, closing my eyes in perfect peace.

"Becky? What do you think? Rebecca!"

Startled, I opened my eyes. "Oh, well, I think it's great. I only wish I'd known your grandfather, so I could've thanked him in person and – "

"What are you talking about?"

Then I remembered Mat hadn't been especially close to his grandfather. "Well, the cabin and all, it being your grandfather's, sort of makes me feel … grateful."

Mat looked annoyed, even angry. I still hadn't learned to read his thoughts the way his mother did. She lived in Maine too, and whenever she came for a visit (once every six months since we'd been married), I felt more at ease with the path our marriage was taking, as she assured me I was on the right track:

"You're dependable, dear," she told me. "Always there for my boy, so flowing and easy, yet …"

I perked up at the Yet Junction.

She took a breath of air that was more like an upside down sigh of relief. "Yet, solid. It's like this: I once rode one of those old trains they keep running in Pennsylvania, you know the ones I'm talking about?"

I ducked my head yes, knotting my thumbs through my fists hopefully.

"Well, those old-fashioned trains keep rolling down those tracks, rolling to remind us of how it used to be, and can be again."

I may have looked confused, but actually I was still hopeful.

"You're the last of an unusual breed of woman, dear, just like those old trains. Destination perfect wife, and – " she gave me a knowing look, "mother. You'll make a superb mother."

Rose has this way of making you feel useful at the very times you feel most in the way of things. I wondered if Mat intended to include his mother in on our plans, but it turned out I was hopelessly off track.

"Good grief, Rebecca. I wasn't talking about the cabin, I was talking about the boat. Our boat."

"Oh, ok. That would be nice, too." I wanted to sound cheery, but I needed a cup of coffee for that. Mat had insisted we stop drinking coffee though. He claimed it was bad for our nerves and health.

On our third day out on the Saint John's River, we finally caught some fish, two which we threw back in because Mat claimed it wasn't sporting to fry up anything so small. "Good girl, you got one!" he said of my first fish, then promptly removed it from the hook, and tossed it back into the river. "Not much bigger than the tears of a giant now, is it?" he said. He leaned over to watch it swam away. "Return to your gods! Away with you!"

I watched it, too, but without ceremony or comment. By this point I was so tired of peanut butter, honey, and turned-brown banana sandwiches, I was inclined not to argue over the size of a giant's tears. But reluctantly, I removed the next fish from my hook when he pronounced it too small as well.

This time though, I returned it to the river gods myself, allowing it to slide gently through my fingers.

"Good girl," he said, disturbing my quiet observation of the small fish first frozen in place at its luck, then swimming furiously away with the river's current and its return to the wilds of precious freedom.

Later, Mat pulled on shore so I could ready our camp while he cleaned the fish he'd caught. Although the fishing wasn't going well so far as I was concerned, the smell and the feel was definitively fishy. Too fishy. I figured that after four days on a muddy river, my bra and panties could use a good washing out. So I washed them in the river like a pioneer woman, feeling my heart beat true and strong as I wrung them out in the bright sunshine, hanging the three pairs of size twelve bikini panties and the two size 36-D bras in the most practical place I could think of: the radio antenna off our boat. And there they flapped in the breeze like so many flags marking the spot of our camp alongside the water. It gave me a sense of purpose and peace to watch them waving at me like that.

As if to salute the flags, the wind picked up and flapped the underwear with a fierce crack. The sound must have carried over to where Mat was cleaning his catch. He stood and turned towards the boat. With a fascinated look, he began walking toward the underwear which now looked like something trying to escape and fly south for the winter.

"What … What on earth are those doing up there?"

"Drying?" My sense of peace was disappearing fast.

"Take them down. Someone will think we're in trouble. They look like SOS banners. They look absurd. Ridiculous. Take them down."

We had three fish to eat that evening, and since Mat had caught them all, he insisted it only right and proper that he cook them as well. Of course, I cut up the onions and mushrooms, gourmet condiments we'd been saving to toss into the pan along with our fresh fish. The fact that the weather had been alternately humid and drizzling at best, plus the fact we forgot to bring enough ice, meant that the onions smelled definitely like onions well before I cut them open. And I cheerfully pointed out to Mat how my simple choice of Safeway's giant fresh mushrooms now closely resembled those of the exotic Shiitake.

But Mat paid no attention. He squatted by his frying pan and fish, giving both his full attention. Maybe more than the mushrooms had shrunk and turned brown in the wild outdoors. A wild man, Mat may have surmised, but I knew he'd never be caught dead in a loincloth. He might espouse the poetry of Robert Bly, but when it came to the imagination of me and Edgar Rice Burroughs, Mat was no Tarzan.

I went back to cutting up my mushrooms more fervently than was necessary.

Mat turned and slowly stood, raising his hands dramatically, and began singing the words to his favorite solo from Phantom of The Opera. "Nighttime sharpens, heightens each sensation … darkness wakes, and stirs imagination! Close your eyes, start adjourning to a strange new world, leave the thoughts of the world you knew behind …"

When he stopped, I clapped politely. The sun had set only moments before, but Mat's animated expressions made it seem as if it were rising once again. "Don't you just love this?" he asked. "Don't you?"

It was obvious he did. So I clapped again.

———

The next day we failed to catch any more fish and decided to depart from our excursion early. Mat's terminal cheerfulness had gone into a state of remission after an attack from the river gods, marking their debut with thunder and lightning, and their finale with mosquitoes and no-see-ums (but sure can-feel-ums), courtesy of a relentless and drizzling rain. Like us, they scorned the size of our fish, too.

I appreciated the remission of Mat's cheerfulness. It picked me right up in spite of the fact that I was also suffering from a lack of sleep.

But as it is with most cases of remission, certain peculiar symptoms die right along with it. In Mat's case, his constant and frenetic energy fizzled out like air from a flattened balloon. He waited too long to pull up anchor, and it was obvious that the tide had decided to leave without us. I guess I could have pulled it up in time myself, and the thought had occurred to me, but as usual I was in that easy chair, fanning the sun and heat from off my face.

Along with the energy went Mat's self-confidence.

"Damn it, damn it, damn it!" His body slumped back against the cabin of his boat, his arms flapping loose at his sides – a grown man pitching a fit. "We're stuck here for another night. And you – " I winced as he stabbed a finger in the air at me, "as usual, you're no help! Fuck a duck." I recovered enough to marvel at his choice of cliché. "Fuck a fucking duck." Now that was turning a phrase. Almost visual. Then Mat slid the length of the cabin wall and sat down hard on the deck.

Resignation was my seat though, and I didn't like how it had settled so easily around Mat's skinny rear end. But his last words settled around my shoulders like the royal cape of a queen, and I was carried off to castles previously known only to my imagination.

At long last, I became that big, brave girl. My soul stretched to proportions once held only by my body. What I did next was like the beating of my heart, the flowing of my blood; it was like the tides of the moons nibbling at my hormones. I was at the mercy of my Celtic roots.

"Oh no we're not. I'll be damned if I'm going to spend another night out here with you." And with that as a cue call, I began tossing everything off the boat.

First to go was Mat's nylon bag filled with clothes and five pairs of boots. He always overpacked and I found the assortment of boots more ridiculous than my assortment of hats. At least I didn't insist on bringing the hats with us. The nylon bag accounted for maybe twenty pounds at the most, but the boat did seem to instantly bob lighter in the water.

Next to go was a smaller box which belonged to the two of us, filled with our mutual rock collection, but which had lately become Mat's rock collection. He'd insisted on pooling our findings long ago. I liked collecting rocks but preferred to name them names I made up myself, unlike Mat, who tagged to each specimen both the common name and the scientific one, until I lost track of the beauty we'd originally discovered upon some glorious mountaintop or beside the quiet waters of a river bed. "Return to your gods! Away with you!" I told the rock collection the box breaking open and spilling the entire collection into the river with many happy plops.

The boat seemed to move a little off the bank, and though it could have been my imagination, the box probably did weigh in at thirty pounds.

Next to go were Mat's books, the ones he'd toted along in a waterproof box. I figured there were enough small river shanties around that some poor and appreciative family would delight in finding such a treasure visited upon their shore. I know I would have. The box of books probably accounted for more than fifty pounds and I felt fifty pounds lighter myself as I tossed them over the side. It was all I could do to keep from cheering out loud. Instead I gave a yelp at the sudden change in body temperature I experienced when next I jumped into the river and began pushing the boat away. "Are you going to help me push this thing, or just stand there looking shocked?"

Mat considered his options a moment, watching me, my blouse floating up around me like a sail, every square inch of me plastered wet and wild like some crazy new twist on a Sports Illustrated Swim Suit Edition combined with a t.v. game show: This Is Your Wife: So What're You Gonna' Do With Her?

Such a question appeared now on Mat's face, and for a brief moment his marvelous control and old-fashioned resolve returned. "No, you go right ahead without me. I am impressed, but I'd rather sit here and look shocked. It's warmer, too."

I gave the boat one last and final shove. It popped off the bank like a cork, and began drifting out towards the middle of the river, a fact that Mat didn't seem to recognize. He was fixated on what had been my next, near simultaneous move, before heaving myself back up onto the deck of the boat. I had ripped my blouse up over my head, baring my large breasts, now swollen larger for a reason known only to me. Drawing my knees up to my chest, I tossed the blouse from the boat into the river where it slowly descended, pulled by the muddy current.

As I watched the blouse disappear, I could feel Mat staring down at my naked body. "Jesus Christ, are you ever getting fat."

I gathered my breasts in my hands, and slowly stood up, wishing I had the nerve to shove him backwards off the boat. "Not as fat as I'm going to get, and I'm going to get really fat. That's a promise." The rage left my body with that matter of fact declaration, and I sat back down on the deck.

Mat was stunned. I was stunned, sitting there with my breasts practically draped across my knees. Yet silence had never sounded so good before. It was a silence that embraced me like the sky up above did the clouds, and I couldn't recall having ever felt quite the way I did just then. Oh, I knew I'd pay for it, and probably in a big way, but I was willing to take the risk. For the first time in my adult life, I'd made a statement worthy of my size.

Mat fired up the Evinrude forty and crouched on bare feet at the stern, his eyes straight ahead and focused on the river. And there he stayed the rest of the way home, positioned at the helm, or so it would have appeared to anyone who might have seen us. But he and I knew better: the one positioned at the helm now, was me.

Luke O'Connor was my best friend and first real love. We'd drift apart, then back again, compelled by inner moons and tides. Soulmates, we called each other, but I was the superstitious one, and believed it best that childhood sweethearts be carried into the future as friends and friends only. I liked to think it had something to do with not wishing more on an important relationship than what was already there.

Luke was a good friend of Dad's too – in fact, Luke and horses were the only two things my father and I ever had in common, besides the same blood.

After Dad died, I shared his reaction to my graduate school aspirations with Luke. "So what did you expect him to say? Your father was a realist, a dyed in the wool cowboy. Probably the only cowboy on the planet who could recite Walt Whitman by heart, but all the same, I don't think he was anyone who could relate to Druids."

"Why not? They were fierce too!"

Luke chuckled. "Fiercely passionate is more like it. Like his daughter."

Luke watched me so closely I'm sure I blushed clear through my tan. Or maybe it was the way he said the word passionate: slow and easy, letting each syllable roll off his tongue in a way that lifted the skin on my body like a wave.

"Whoooo, it's cold in here." I stood up quickly and reached for our mugs to refill them with coffee. But Luke stopped me.

Glancing down at his hand on my arm, I pulled away. "Well, I do declare, Slim, all this talk about cowboys and Druids is enough to make a gal go toxic on testosterone." Drama classes aside, I always could do a fairly good imitation of a Texas drawl.

But Luke's drawl was no imitation. His was for real, straight from the Panhandle. "And how do you spell … testosterone, my dear?"

I pretended to be shocked. "Ooooh, and aren't you the flirt?"

Luke rocked his chair back on two legs. He seemed to hang in the air there, both hands shoved inside his front pockets, a smile light as a cloud upon his face.

"Oooh? Since when does a big strong gal like you say oooh? What was that, some sad excuse for a great barbaric yawp?"

Dodging his hand as it snaked out at me, I threatened to pour my coffee on him, but he didn't flinch. So I sat down and pretended to study the designs on the table cloth instead.

"C'mon, tell me. How do you spell it?"

Pushing back in my chair, I pulled a mock hat down over my eyes and did my Calamity Jane imitation. "Why mister ..." I heaved my sock-clad feet on top of the table like I was wearing a pair of heavy boots. "I don't spell it. My mama raised me to be a lady."

Luke had given a genuine, great barabaric yawp. "And my mama raised me to love ladies. So pray tell, Becky Lee, why are you afraid of me: darling?"

Afraid of Luke? He wasn't what scared me. Luke used an indepth background in linguistics to help women improve their fates in the shark-infested waters of the business world. "I love women," he said often. "Like to see them run the whole dang planet, myself. Heck, I just love them."

That's what scared me. The thought that all those women might come to love him back. It was a fear that turned out to have a twist all its own, thanks to Mat. A fear I came to call the Belly Dance of Life.

---

Around the time of the river mutiny, Luke convinced me to take a test. He suggested that I write down five major events in my life that were positive and had had good results, and then to write down five more that were negative and had had negative results. It didn't matter what age I was, or what I might have been doing. All that mattered was that they be significant for me.

"Might rope yourself a connection or two, darling," he said.

"You do this kind of stuff in your business workshops?"

"Yeah, works for them, too. Some fall back in love with their husbands, others with their best girlfriends ..." I pretended to look shocked, and Luke smiled. "And some decide to like themselves for the first time in their lives."

"Why such reactions to something as simple as this?"

"Because it's simple, and stuff shows up as new information that might not have shown up before."

"So what do they do with this stuff, this information? And I like myself, just fine, thank-you," I added quickly.

"Depends. I remember one woman divorced her husband, bought a sailboat, then sailed straight to Hawaii. She's been living there ever since. Every now and then I get a postcard."

Yeah, I bet he did. I bet he got lots of postcards. As for sailing, I'd already had more than my share of boats.

Just as I was writing down the fifth most significant event in my life (I finished quickly with the negative ones), I was overwhelmed by nausea. I made it to the bathroom in time, but missed my mark. Generally speaking, projectile vomiting signifies one of two things: disease or health. I retrieved pen and paper – the only things in the bathroom not covered in vomit – and sat down on the coldness of the linoleum to write what was the only event significant to me from that moment on.

I, Rebecca Lee Mason, was going to give birth to a baby.

It by far superseded anything positive I'd already written on the list. But what I didn't know at the time was how it would become significant for Mat, too. He placed it at the top of his most negative list. Which was when I began sleeping in the guest room of my own house.

It wasn't much after that, when I did, in fact, rope myself a connection or two.

———

"Don't be so melodramatic, he's just anxious," said my mother when I told her how Mat didn't seem to want a baby. Our baby. "Give him time, he'll come around," said Rose, Mat's mother. Then, with that odd sighing sound of hers, she added, "He was an only child after all. He's never been displaced before."

Pregnancy has a way of making the most low-key personality melo-dramatic, and since I'm anything but low-key, Mom's advice was a little alienating. What did Mat have to be anxious about anyway?

Maybe Rose was right. Time. I could give Mat that much, as I had plenty of it now, having decided to temporarily drop out of my doctorate program. I was waiting for the baby, so I could wait for Mat to get used to the idea as well. There was no reason for him to feel displaced. The swell of my belly, with skin so taut you could bounce a quarter off it, was doing enough displacing for the two of us.

As it turned out, it was Mat who performed the art of displacement with a finesse that left me breathless. The afternoon of my five month checkup, I decided to stop in to surprise him. But he surprised me first. I deliber-ately waited till long after his students had filed out of the classroom. Then smoothing the folds of silk down around my bulging belly (a new maternity smock and recent gift from Mat), I took a deep breath, opened the door to Mat's room, and quietly walked in.

The only good thing about endings are the small thoughts of hope wing-ing their way from a broken heart – like baby birds poking blind heads towards the sky for nourishment. Thoughts that eventually take over and crowd out of the nest any lingering thoughts of despair.

Mat always was an attentive teacher, and close to his students in ways I found admirable. But the small, very thin, and very young woman snuggled up in Mat's arms obliterated all boundaries I knew concerning attentiveness.

The woman kept trying to brush aside my husband's cowlick, which insisted on bouncing right back into place each time she did. She giggled, and Mat pulled her closer.

Watching the two happy bodies, my own body remembered how much it missed being loved. It was like having a movie take place in your nervous system with the sound turned off. But the language of the body has its own sound. It's a language that demands to be heard, no matter how painful or how late, so that what you end up hearing is the beat of your own heart and the voice of your own soul as it rides up beside you.

I'd come to accept the place where Mat's and my relationship had gone to, and then one day I called Luke. We drove to Dad's old place of business, and mounting up on an old bay mare I'd known since I was tiny, that I knew wouldn't dream of spilling me and my new pregnancy to the ground, the two of us rode out along the ocean. We rode right up into the sand dunes that no one seemed to know about but us, and it was there that we almost stopped being riding partners, and went on to being something more.

It was the exact same feeling I'd get when my body hasn't known a horse in a long time and my mind has come to a place where it thinks it has outgrown the body's need there, only to discover upon riding along the ocean how wrong I am. And how happy I am to come up against such a wrong coming right again – right up and rolling beneath me, bridging the muscles of my thighs and the extension of the reins talking my soul to the soul of a horse through hands that somehow manage to stay strong, stay gentle, in spite of any calluses life might hand out.

With timing more perfect than Shakespeare himself, my father's words slipped into my mind. "Ride the horse in the direction it's going, my Celtic cowgirl."

The woman gave up on Mat's cowlick, and started nibbling at his ear. She gushed a couple of inaudible somethings, and then in an unmistakably husky voice, a tone that carried through her whole body and caused mine to shudder, she spoke loud enough for me to hear. "You rascal you." Mat leaned closer – as if he could get any closer. "You're such a pistol, that's what you are, Matthew Mason. A sure-fired pistol."

I pulled on the resources of every drama class I'd ever attended. And with the best Texas drawl I could muster, I delivered the punch line: "Let's hope you're quick on the draw then, for it appears as if he's ready to take it out of his holster."

Then I turned and walked off into the sunset, or whatever else it is you say when an ending takes place in a bad western you probably never should have taken a part in to begin with.

---

Maybe it's my height, but I never seem to be able to see what's right before my eyes until it's almost too late. It's as if I get information first through my toes, and then it has to travel all the way up to my brain, and only then does it fall back down against my heart and stay there.

Lovers learn things about each other that friends can never know.

Holding my face in his hands, Luke said, "I once read where an Irish sage believed there were three things a man never forgets: his first girlfriend, a devoted teacher, and a great horse."

Feeling big as a horse myself, I didn't answer straight off. Instead I took hold of one of his hands and turned it palm up to study it. "Hmm. You've a long lifeline, and an even longer memory."

"I never knew cowgirls read palms."

"Celtic cowgirls do. We can tell time by the moon as well. And I never knew you lived in a cabin by the ocean."

"We don't live in cabins, we live in here." He pulled his palm away and brushed it like a feather across the skin between my breasts, then moved it along til it settled softly on my belly. "And what moonth are we in now?"

"What moonth are we in?" I lumbered up into some semblance of a sitting position. "Moonth, huh? You word play fiend, you. Well, did you know that not only do I read palms, I do astrological charts as well?"

And slowly, exploring those places that only lovers can, I began charting the length of his body, and when I reached his secret place, I knew more than the moon could ever want to know.

"Your Sagitarrius is rising. Again."

Luke pulled me close, even closer than soul-mates, and tenderly thumped my watermelon of a belly. Then placing his ear against my skin, he listened for the life that was pulsating a beat all its own. "And your belly is dancing, dear heart."

———

Like it or not, certain men stand out in a woman's life. And three stand out in mine.

Make that four. It's a boy.

# CRAZY: A PATSY CLINE STORY

It was March fifth, 1963, I was eight years old, and Patsy Cline had just died. I wasn't exactly eight, my birthday falls on the eighth, but since Patsy herself had told me it was my lucky number (eight), that's what I told the reporter.

"I'm eight years old today," I said in answer to his first question. He already knew my name and a bit about who I was. I was Patsy Cline's best friend. Young, but heck, it took young to figure out that Patsy needed a friend, needed a best friend more than anything else. It didn't matter to me and it sure the hell didn't matter to Patsy how old I was or wasn't.

Well … I wasn't quite eight. It was Mrs. Price who insisted early on in the third grade that we round off all numbers to the nearest whole integer. Since three days shy of a year seemed a heck of a lot closer to the number eight than did 361 to the number seven, I lied about my age. But when the reporter showed up at my house and asked all those questions, and that one question in particular, I guess I was fixated on the happy aspect of the number itself, and this year's birthday falling on the eighth of March besides made this uncommon coincidence especially lucky.

In hindsight I guess you could say I wanted to hurry the luck along, and that I jumped at the chance of taking on the age of eight three days early because I was impatient for luck. You could even say I was starved for luck. You could say a lot of things in hindsight.

Sure enough, the reporter was suspicious, the insinuation being – well, it was obvious. "You're eight? You're Patsy Cline's best friend is what they say, and … you're … eight … years … old. Well … Imagine that."

It was one thing for me to lie about my age, but to hear it lied out loud from a total stranger, well, that made me squirm to say the least. The reporter saw my discomfort and grinned with pure pleasure. He whipped a pencil out from behind his ear and pointed the eraser end at me and wiggled it in the air. I didn't like that. No one was going to erase nothing out of my life – certainly not my friendship with Patsy. I decided right then and there that lying to that damn reporter was nothing less than an act of dignity. And that his reporting was nothing less than pure meanness, the insinuation being that no matter when my birthday, it was uncommonly strange that someone my size, my age, would be touted as the great Patsy Cline's best friend.

Age, in the adult world, seems to be a concluding factor for a lot of things. At that instance it was all the more so – which I'll admit, was another reason for lying. Besides, the reporter already knew everything about me except my age and so I repeated myself: "It's true: I'm standing smack at eight today."

For the first time in my life I was older than the number of days in a week. I doubted I would ever feel this way again – at least not till I was thirty-two when it could be said I was older than the days in a month. But that birthdate so far off in the future seemed further away than the stars and not nearly so bright as claiming the entire integer of eight for my very own. For the first time in my life also, I lied about my age. It was to be the last time I lied about my age, too, because the reporter's next question, thrown at me casual yet certain, as silent and surprising as a knife cut, was this one: "So, hey kid, how'd you feel when you got the news about Patsy's death?"

It was a stupid question. It completely caught me off guard, but the reporter didn't know that, and I sure the heck didn't let on I didn't know … that. I just stood there dumb as a post like they say, but then I'd been struck all deaf and dumb and numb all over by the reporter's question. Like I said it was a stupid question to ask anyone, let alone a seven year old child pretending to be all of eight, a child who'd loved Patsy more than she ever could have loved her own mother.

If she'd even had a mother.

The reporter stood there, his pencil aimed in my direction like a weapon, waiting to see which way I'd go first before he launched it back at his writing pad. He stared at me, scrunching up his face like he was trying to hold back some kind of clown's smile, a smile anything but proper given the moment. Not that he knew a damn thing about this moment, or any of the other moments that were to mark my life from this one onwards, but he probably suspected something. After all, he was one of them; he was a reporter whose unearthly job it was to report on the lives of people who were fully alive and living. "It's what they like to do, write about folks like us because they're all dead inside themselves and it makes 'em nuts to be left out of it all," Patsy told me. "The only thing they like to report on even better is if they find out you've gone and died. Man oh man, do they ever love to write about that." She went on to say how they not only write about what comes out of your mouth, they write about what doesn't too, making stuff up to suit their headlines; or they write about what comes over your face and what all they think that's supposed to mean.

But I'd been taught well by Patsy: I didn't flinch. I held my head high and looked him square in the face. I wasn't going to react like some kind of seven year old baby, I was claiming my lucky number on the spot!

I don't know what it was came over me next, but it was as if by reaching into the future like that – stretching out with the self-contained fury of a barn kitten turned cat and faced with the ill intentions of a cur dog – I was able to sum up the courage to smile at that man. Smile sweetly even. I believe it was the perfect smile to aim back at his weapon of a writing pencil, a bold and brave eight year old smile brought on by a moment. A particular moment, one that was to define the rest of my life.

I'd never felt this way before: I was too scared to be scared.

Maybe it was the memory of Patsy's voice and how I knew I'd never hear it again except on the radio, or maybe it was something I will never figure out, but whatever it was I just knew I wasn't going to start off the rest of my life by letting Patsy down now.

"You know how that one song goes by Patsy? That particular one song? The words and all? Crazy? That's how I felt. I just felt … crazy."

# For Pete's Sake

I won't forget the way the light spilled out from the barn door later on that evening, the way it spilled out from a single light bulb shining out from the oldest building in that part of Texas at the dark clouds and the night coming on, winds blowing, buckets rattling, you roaring at the kids, you …. I won't forget the way the wind and the rain blew up against your face sideways, or how your horse pitched his body hard to one side so quiver quick – you should have gone sideways like the weather yourself. Instead you just breathed into that saddle, grinned into the leather like it was your own skin, but then I suppose it was your own skin right then right there.

And when you turned to go in out of the rain, inside where all the people were, you paused and looked back towards the night. I won't forget how the weather dripped off your hat as you stood in the door with the light reaching out soft for your shoulder, and me out front in a moonless dark looking back in at you. You, dang it. All the time always, it was you.

Then what was it you told the audience later on that evening? I remember. You said this: "See there now? See how she came two steps towards me … unasked for?"

And that very willing audience nodded its collective head like so many cattle, but then they figured you were talking about the horse.

# MEANEST MAN

Mom says that T.K. Stone has taught her more about working horses, persistence, and trust than any other human being. What she doesn't tell folks (simply because she never knew I was hiding right there in the barn all along) is that he taught her who to trust.

That never was T.K. Stone.

I knew he wasn't to be trusted the first day I saw him lay eyes on my mother at a party. He'd been undeniably drunk, and whenever he thought my mother wasn't looking he'd stare at her chest. Since Arlin has the bosom of a ten year old boy, I found that to be ridiculous, not to mention downright rude to the timid blonde who was his date that evening.

That's the way I saw it then and that's the way I see it now, and I'd be willing to bet a king sized pack of M&M Peanuts candy that that's how the horses see it too.

So if Mom has any brains at all she'll figure out right as rain that the day T.K. threatened to kick her out of his training barn – keeping that roan filly she broke in and put the best ninety days riding time in on for himself – that that was the meanest thing T.K. ever did.

Mean. Deceitful. Heck! It was downright hateful, and I clapped both hands over my mouth to keep from cheering out loud. After all I was hiding right there in the empty stall they used to keep Old Red in before T.K. sold him to Ozzie's for their fish feed manufacturing company, when my mother told T.K. what she really thought of it all. Mom only weighs in at ninety-five pounds, five pounds less than I do at age twelve, but her words packed fighting weight that day.

"T.K.? That filly's not ready for you to swing a leg on over yet, and you know it. You'll ruin her if you start spinning circles on her now. Leave her here with me a few days more and then you can have at her, T.K.," she said.

She sounded more worried than angry. I scooted down further in the stall, hoping I wouldn't be discovered, but curiosity made me brave. Spotting a bale of hay which had fallen down from its perch on top of the others, I tiptoed silent as an Indian across the stall floor towards it. It was big and bulky, but I managed to roll it up against the barn wall to stand on. Perfect. And then I peered out towards the riding arena where Mom was with the filly and Terence K. Stone.

"I mean it, T.K. This horse isn't ready for you to swing a leg on over yet."

T.K. was standing a couple yards away from her. He just tipped his hat at her, the one with the baby coonskin hatband, and shook his head, grinning. T.K.'s the only person I know who can grin and grit his teeth all at the same time, his eyes leering right at my mom's chest to rattle her confidence some. He spit out two words only. "I'm ready."

Then he jerked his head towards the training barn, his eye falling on Old Red's stall window, and for a moment I thought he'd spotted me. But then I realized that the motion was meant for my mom, the top flyweight horse trainer in all of Montana, to go and get T.K.'s personal saddle for the roan filly. T.K. undid the cinch on Mom's saddle in a second, tossing it roughly to the ground.

I figured Mom would let him have it then, but one look told me it didn't seem likely. Why, that grinning goofball would have her saddling up horses for him to ride into prize monies and glory for the rest of her fool life if Mom were to let him keep scooping her horses like that!

But Mom just stared at him, big-eyed and scared some, and at first I wondered if she really would break down and cry in front of the meanest man alive. Then, quick as lightning, I saw the change come over her face. Her eyes went dark as a sudden summer storm cloud, and the big-eyed look that took up her whole face took on a considerable change. She looked downright mean. And with both palms shoved flat beneath her armpits, she barricaded herself against T.K. Stone.

She stood there firm as a thistle and twice as wiry, exactly like the champion cowgirl I knew her to be. And then, she spit two words right back – and spat for real at the scuffed over leather toes of T.K. Stone.

"I quit," she said evenly, and so softly I leaned forward and nearly fell off the bale of hay, I was straining my ears so hard to be sure I'd heard her right.

Those were her words all right, and T.K. heard them too, his eyes fixed on the toes of his boots now instead of my mom's chest.

He searched the pockets of his faded black denim Lee Rider's shirt for the pack of Marlboro cigarettes he'd left back at the house. The way I knew his mind to work, he'd probably left them there on purpose – one more errand for my mother to go run for him, but I kind of doubted he'd ask her to go run it right then.

"Gawd damn woman." He swore under his breath so that only the barn, the dust, and I heard him. Mom thumbed her nose at him from the safety of several yards away. A good sign, I thought. The fact is I know Mom can always out run T.K. even if Montana claims she can't out ride him.

"I'll throw your ass out of this training barn and off'a' my team before you'll ever quit me," he said.

Yet I couldn't help but notice how he mumbled it so Mom could barely hear him. For a second it almost sounded as if he really needed her after all, even liked her a little. I never would have figured that before. Of course I never have understood why all the horses come running to him either, but they do. Those fool horses don't seem to know any better, they just come running every time T.K. whistles, whether he's got grain with him or not.

Standing out there in the middle of that great big arena he did look worried, even lonesome. But not for long!

"Don't ever come back then. Be sure and take that kid with you, too!" he yelled, picking up a rock like he might chuck it at her.

I ducked down from the window, and Rambo, T.K.'s prize winning Quarter Horse stud, snorted anxiously from his stall down the aisle.

"I got men all over this state wanting to pay me for what all I give you for free, goddamn your flat ass anyway!" he roared. "I'm the one taught you everything worth knowing about horses … pay you good wages … put a roof over your head, the kid's too. And this is how you treat me in return?"

Hey, far as I knew, he didn't pay her but a few dollars, and he didn't give her that till she was well on her way out the door to buy groceries. Besides all that, T.K. eats three times more than Mom and I put together.

"You leave now, don't come back. I'm warning you," he said.

A rodeo announcer once called this old bull, rattlesnakes and cactus mean. I felt it to be the perfect description of T.K. Stone. And his next words, hurled at my mom like poison, only confirmed the rattlesnake part in my mind.

"Get on outta' here then! Take that kid with you too – she ain't nothing like any kid I ever expected to have ..."

It was right at this point that I felt slightly confused, but I shook my head at the words he'd just shouted, and I listened on.

"I know there's tomboys, but she beats all, I tell you – she's a pain! And you, who needs you anyway? You: a woman, ha! You'll never get anywhere in this business without my help, I expect you to remember that much, Blondie. This is Texas, and Texas don't hold by women with no loyalty, sister," he sneered.

Mom turned and began the walk I'd always prayed for: the walk away from T.K. Stone and Stonehill Ranch. Right then I began planning out our new life, a life without T.K. Stone. I figured that the only thing we'd miss – the only thing I'd miss – would be the horse called Rambo, but naturally he'd have to stay behind with T.K. After all he was T.K.'s horse. As for the other horses that flooded in on a regular basis, I'd miss them too, but ...

But then Mom stopped suddenly three strides later, pivoting lightly on the heel of her boot, her face with that scrunched up look she gets when she's thinking hard about something.

"Texas? T.K., you said 'Texas.' We're not in Texas any more," she said. "Don't you remember? We're not in Texas, darling. We're in Montana."

She spoke like she was talking to some confused or very small child. It was disgusting to say the least. I wondered just how many years more I could hope to keep her safe from men like T.K. if she worked any harder than she already did at playing dumb.

T.K. shrugged his jacket up higher on his shoulders, his thumbs hooked in the belt loops of his 501 jeans. He pretended to pout – as if rattlesnakes could pout. He toed each Durango boot in the dirt like a schoolboy, rolling that dang rock around in his hand like it was some kind of diamond ring or otherwise precious stone. Then damn if he didn't begin tapping his boot like

he was keeping beat to a tune, slapping one denim clad ،
fashion, as if Mom were some fool dog.

But it didn't fool me.

The dust rose up from the arena grounds like a smoke warning, and damn if his next words didn't raise the hair on the back of my neck to boot.

"Well ya' see how it is now, hon," he said, Texas in his voice, and Texas in the slouch of his hips. He tipped his hat back further on his head and I studied that baby coonskin hatband like it was my own skin.

"I'm lost without you babes, you should know that by now," he said sweetly. Too sweetly. "Can't keep track of what day it is let alone know where I am if you ain't by my side, baby doll."

I saw the scrunched up look on Mom's face give way to a smile that made my eyes water. But it was the words which came next from T.K. Stone himself that nearly caused my head to spin right off my shoulders.

"Why do you think after all this time I came back for yuse two, huh, baby doll? Why, once upon a time we made the cutest kid in all of Texas together, our very own little girl, Rumer. She's the spitting image of the best parts of me and you, babe. So tell me: did you think I could stay away forever from the cutest gal alive and my own child?" he said, pushing his hat back on his head at a cocky angle, moving confidently towards my mother.

Spitting image of the best part of who? Our little girl Rumer? Oh no. I was Rumer. So this was it? This was the reason why my mom worked hard as she did, and practically for free? This tobacco stained, phony grinning, chain-smoking fool was …. No. No way! It couldn't be. This man was my very own flesh and – I could hardly stand the thought, let alone state the words out full in my mind.

The breakfast I'd eaten that morning rumbled, threatening to leave my stomach. I saw stars too, the kind that make your head feel weird. What I'd just learned made me want to scream out loud, but I wasn't about to give myself away in so undignified a manner. So I kicked the barn wall instead. I kicked it hard like Rambo. They were both so entangled in one another's arms like burrs on a saddle blanket, I figured they'd just think it was Rambo anyway.

*The Losing of These Things*

Then just like that, Mom starts back towards Stonehill's training barn to get the saddle for Old Sperm Bank himself, my blood father only, and the meanest man in Whatside County.

# Ragnar's Lincoln

That time I saw Ragnar Blue, he rode in from behind a cloud of purple haze: dust raised from the fall of that damn mule, and the pain that filtered everything through my eyes as nothing short of black and blue.

That he was there, I was certain, though not as certain about breaking in any more mules. For I had just hit the ground with the force of a kamikaze pilot, a force so hard I felt separated from my own body, and sorely wished I had been.

He appeared to be suspended in space, his small form dangling in a blue Montana sky, and just where he'd come from I hadn't a clue, nor a point of reference. Nothing told me nothing, and the pain was such that I questioned my very eyes, but there was just no holding back what I knew from within.

For I knew beyond the shadows, sensed it in spite of the doubts, that the figure riding towards me without his wheelchair was my son, Ragnar Blue.

I didn't shout. I didn't say a word. I couldn't have if I'd tried. But not even the pain that pinned my muscles into a breakdance independent of my mind could stop the sounds of happy that I heard the whispers making. Whispers claiming I'd been right all along, that this boy they swore would never walk, would never talk, was sitting straight up as an arrow on a horse.

And he was riding closer.

He rode as if embraced within the arms of air and sunshine only, and clouds, clouds soft and giant riding guard from above. And even as I hurt, even as I strained my fool eyes at the figure riding towards me, I knew what I had always known: I'd been hurting all along. There was no need to reflect on whether I had broken more than mere dirt and ground.

I was broken in many places; I ached in every limb as if on fire, but the small silhouette riding against the sun's setting behind Shadow Mountain and that crazy barn up ahead – a barn which up till now hadn't even been there in the half acre pasture where I broke in horses for a living – cooled the fever, soothing every hurt I'd ever known.

And I smiled as Rags rode closer.

He was riding that horse as sure as the day he flew the kite himself. Together, me and Rags, we sent that kite soaring above them all. And when it crashed amidst the stares of strangers who looked away, I shook a fist at the sky, cursing God's wind, broken strings, and anything else I could think of, too.

But as I bent down to comfort my son, the kite took off like a colt, the wind blew the tears dry on a turned-happy face, and Rags squealed with delight, his hand clamped tight to the string of his bucking wind horse.

After the kite rode up in the sky, another child, a little girl who had been watching with curiosity even as the others turned away, clapped her hands too, and walked over to stand shyly next to Rags. Leaning one elbow on the arm of his wheelchair, she boldly hailed each passerby, directing all who came near, "See? He can do it, he can fly a kite!"

So now he was flying solo once more, his small form swaying with the dance of his horse. How he'd managed to climb aboard the animal himself, I didn't know, nor could I hardly imagine, but he was riding all the same.

But that barn … the barn confused me. It stood there solid and real, worn through at the ribs, brushed white like bare bone by the sun, and where the light bounced through and off the other side, it gave it a second cover: a fierce shield of Rose Madder and Cobalt Blue. Colors to embarrass the most eccentric of farmers.

But when I looked away for that damn mule who'd been grazing sly and fat – grazing like grass was all that mattered in the world – there was no mule.

In the mule's place stood a man, a long-lanky and very solemn stranger, wrapped up in an old fashioned black coat, a stove pipe hat raised tall upon his head. His frame seemed entirely made of bones, bones surrounded by the shyest amount of flesh, and his shoulders slumped over and forward. Forward in a way more certain than my future was with mules.

The man appeared to me, familiar. Yet I knew I'd never seen him in person before. And then given my dilemma – not to mention my most inglorious position on the ground – I didn't know if I was seeing anything at all beyond my own pain.

Yet still he leaned strong and silent against a single barn door, and I had to look hard.

Tall as old growth forest he was, all shaded in parts like a cedar tree planted firmly on a hill, every root running deep in solitude.

I shut my eyes tight for a moment, and opened them back up – with much resistance – to the whispers once more.

Ragnar Blue was still riding towards me, slowly, riding to test my heart again. Riding to find his place among the men, his spastic and twisted body with a beat all its own, traveling in time like a carousel horse.

And he, too, kept his eyes on the stranger.

The man drew himself up more long and lanky than before, complete with this sad, sad look which seemed more and more familiar.

It was a look belonging to old widows, and mules pulling vegetable carts. A look belonging to old generals and all men who have lost their wars. A look belonging to the one they called Abraham Lincoln.

He touched a finger to his nose and solemnly nodded his head in my direction. I nodded back in return. (What else could I do?) And though the colors were slightly fading around that barn door, Rags and the stranger appeared more sharply defined than a pen and ink sketch. And I vowed to capture on paper forever the pictures I was seeing. I would be afraid no more.

For there was something distinctly safe in the way the stranger's eyes met my own, eyes bridged by brows dark and shaggy as two unclipped poodle puppies, and twice as friendly, sadness and all. And when he spoke, I heard a voice I'd assumed to be God's timbre alone.

"No more mules, daughter, for that is how I think of you: Daughter." He spoke kindly enough.

Rags sat his horse tight as a tick, his hands clasped together as if in prayer: a tiny steeple mounted on a saddlehorn. His legs hung thin as reins down around the horse's sides, and the animal shifted from hoof to hoof without moving in any particular direction. But instead of watching me, my boy's eyes were commanded by the stranger's. And I listened soft and close. I listened for the first time since I'd been breaking mules.

"You've been hurt and shamed as well," said the man. "But the shame doesn't belong on you. Mules can't have children, and that's what makes them so mean and jealous."

The very mention of jealous mules brought to mind those members of the Rock Solid Christian Assembly of Jesus Christ – and not the mule who had thrown me to the ground. It was like my senses weren't my own, and for one brief moment I knew fear again. And found myself wishing to be back along the banks of east Humbug Creek, listening outside the doors to the church. Or even inside, where I'd never belonged in the first place, and never would.

Inside and singing for once in my life, singing with those fool ass folk who make up the bulk of the church. Members who were mostly embittered women, women without a single child left among them. Women who each year rejected my paintings for the annual church bazaar, informing me that God hadn't forgiven me just yet. But that He would. Perhaps soon.

So I kept on painting, offering up my gifts of pictures every year, hoping one day they would choose one and give a place to me and my boy in the church.

Oh, I had my place all right! My place was to be an example of sin both past and present made manifest in the child who was my precious own: my very own flesh and blood. Although I worked hard at pretending not to know.

But I knew. And when I painted the picture of Ragnar Blue, my fragile and broken-winged bird of an angel's glory, they destroyed it. They held it up before the church, claiming some fool notion that it was an evil thing, and that it would never hang on the walls of a holy place. They claimed it to be one last barrier between me and true glory.

Yet it was instead for me a bridge. I would make my way back, alone. I would pretend no more. I closed my eyes; I closed my heart. I left the church on Humbug Creek; I left the women. And went back to working horses, or a mule from time to time, because the mules brought more money.

And for the most part, no shame.

As if reading my mind, the man nodded his head, the slightest mention of a smile hiding behind the finger he'd pressed across his lips. He sat down sudden-like in the dirt like a playing child, drawing those long, long legs to his chest in the story-telling fashion he'd been famous for. And that's when I knew it was him. It was Abraham Lincoln.

He saw me start and move back again. He spoke to the place where I felt caught in between; he held me close right there.

"You've got the idea, and gifts besides." He watched me carefully. "Why look at all this," and he waved his arms big as God all around him. "You're blessed, and you don't know it. I'm going to let you keep the barn, but no more mules, daughter. Just paint the pictures as they come along. Don't throw them to the ground with mules. Use the pictures. And that boy of yours will ride along fine."

And then for him, the sadness seemed to return, as his voice trailed off: "Most folks are about as happy as they make up their minds to be."

Then he snapped both thumb and finger in front of an amazing face, and the long-lanky, and so very solemn Lincoln disappeared along with the barn door, though the barn itself remained at the far side of the pasture, open and dark.

I leaned up on one elbow, crying softly at the pain, but crying more at the pain melting away from my heart, my unforgiving heart. My head felt struck by lightning, but I had never seen more clearly.

And then the lights flashed out like stars one by one, and all was darker than the most moonless night.

But not before I caught sight once more of Ragnar Blue, his small form softer than the most pleasant dream, distant in a gentle way, a mere shadow nestled in the crook of a saddle. And he was riding a horse, Rags was. And he was riding towards me again.

# SAND CRABS DANCING SIDEWAYS

Years ago if you had asked me, his only son, I'd have told you that J.J. Flick was a very hard man, that he was born mean and determined to stay that way. I'd have told you about the time I wrote a prize winning essay in high school entitled Hard Versus Tough, and how he refuted there being any distinction between the two. It was a point of view he insisted on having right up through the moment I read the essay on the auditorium stage, and returned to my seat beside him accompanied by resounding applause.

When I returned to my seat, he leaned over to whisper in my ear. I assumed he was going to give me a word or two of praise, albeit reluctantly, but praise all the same, since the audience had received my words as if I were reading their sentiments out loud exactly. I even leaned in at his shoulder to make it easy on him.

"You wouldn't know tough if it walked up and bit you on the ass. Tough's nothing but a state of mind and hard's a decision you haven't had to make yet. A decision that just might determine how tough you really are."

As if his words weren't shocking enough, he had to go and shock me further by planting a kiss on my cheek, not an action well received by a fifteen year old boy. I wiped the kiss off my face like I was swatting a fly, yet it didn't take me more than a moment to know that once again my father had stolen the show.

Back in 1969 I had just finished up my last year of high school on the Big Island in the state of Hawaii where I was born, and where J.J. Flick ran the most successful construction contracting business in the Hawaiian Islands. It was then, shortly after my mother died, that Flick decided it was time for me to start showing signs of following in his footsteps.

The fact that I had no intentions of following in his footsteps did nothing to sway him from his purpose. I didn't know what I'd do, I just knew it wouldn't be what he was doing – the ongoing slaughter of a precious island ecology. An insight I stupidly related in those very words to my father, which only served to make my life miserable and Flick more determined than ever for me to become the next J.J. Flick.

"Starting with sales, boy!" he said. "We're to sponsor the Hawaii Cowman's Association's tenth annual cutting horse contest this year, kid, and I'm giving you the most important job of all … enrollee, got it? Now here's what you do …"

What I did was go out and talk with less successful men in the construction business who owed my father favors – either that or Flick was counting coup. The distinctions weren't always clear, but the mood was: everyone seemed scared to death of my father. My job was to convince the men to pledge X amount of money towards the prize kitty. Money was the only prize worth going after according to Flick.

Although Dad assured me that "ever' one of those buggers will want to play in this game, kid, it's damn important for their business futures!", my sense of the feelings coming from the men I spoke with didn't exactly exude the essence of Win/Win.

There was one company in particular, United Fencing of Hawaii. They were a new franchise that sold fencing material to island ranchers and were more than a little anxious upon discovering that they were talking to J.J. Flick's son.

By this time I had engaged several companies in pledge money towards the amount that Flick had committed to raise that year. I knew my father to be a man driven to win at everything and anything he got himself into, but since I'd met the target quota he'd set for me, I thought I could simply talk with the men from that point on. In short, do some much needed PR work for Dad.

No doubt he'd be working with them in the future. For not only was he a forerunner of the mass mushrooming of Sheratons and namebrand hotel industries sprouting up and down the South Kohala coastline, his most recent venture was developing five and ten acre parcels for gentlemen ranchers. Those who romanticized themselves as paniolos: Hawaiian Cowboys.

But Flick wasn't impressed with my quota.

"Why the hell didn't you close those guys when you had the chance to, son? Why, they're handling the biggest sales of hog wire and straight line fencing in the islands!" he said. "Frankly, I'm disappointed in you, Josh, but not to worry. We'll just drive back down to Kona and close them together. Heck – it's their checkmate."

By the time we drove back to Kailua-Kona, a once small fishing town on the southwest side of the Big Island, I wasn't clear on just how Flick would handle the situation, but I knew he'd think of something.

Sure enough, Flick zeroed right in on the man who counted most: Tim Daniels, the anxious regional manager for United Fencing who was fresh out of business school and a small town in Pennsylvania. And he'd heard enough stories about my father to give double meaning to the common courtesy of handshaking.

"Glad to meet you, Tim …. hate to be brief, but I believe we've a misunderstanding here. See, my son Josh here – " Dad pulled me out from behind him, throwing an arm around my shoulders – "was under the impression that you'd be tickled pink to sponsor the third prize trophy money this year," he said. Then, with one of his infamous pregnant pauses, he gazed hard at another man who was standing behind the cash register. "But your right hand man there, or so he claimed he was to my boy here, claims otherwise."

Daniels shifted uncomfortably from one foot to the other, glancing back sharply at the dumbfounded assistant manager. Daniels began to speak, but Flick cut him short.

"Ok. Folks do change their minds sudden-like, don't they? It breaks my heart to have you feel this way, but I understand priorities. Do I ever! 'Course now, rumor has it that Triple A's thinking of moving a franchise out here themselves. You're a trailblazer, you know," he said, strong traces of Oklahoma gaining with every word spoken. "Just new enough in island economics to still shine. Bet your boss hasn't even tossed out the box he sent you over in yet, has he?"

Flick laughed aloud at his own joke, and I had all I could do to keep from passing out in shame.

Flick popped the palm of one hand with a fist, deliberately silent for several drawn out moments. "Well, I know how these things are, so don't you worry none. 'Course now I have to walk into that group of men tonight … big strong family men … paniolo blood in ever' one of 'em … and tell fifty cutters there won't be any third prize trophy money this year because we had a misunderstanding with all of —"

Tim Daniels cleared his throat with a sound resembling a yelp. "Uh, well now, sir, we've thought this over and have decided to meet your pledge challenge after all." Daniel's body jerked involuntarily. "We think it's a good cause," he added weakly.

"Congratulations!" boomed Flick, striding forward and slapping the man on the shoulder, reaching over the counter for the other employee who stepped back as if dodging a left jab, his eyes shifting from Dad's to his boss's.

Flick, unperturbed, reached into a pocket of his jacket and pulled out what appeared to be rodeo script. "Here, give these to the wife and kids. Have some chili on me," he said, throwing an arm around Daniel's shoulders. "How about giving me a tour around your place here? Josh, you wait in the truck … I'll meet you for the road shortly."

The moment the two of them were out of sight, I turned sheepishly to the assistant manager.

"I'm real sorry about all of this," I said. "I don't know why he does stuff like that," was all I could think to add.

"It's not your problem," the man said, shaking his hand out to the side in a half-hearted wave of dismissal. "But hey, that's sure some father you got there."

"Yeah. Tell me about it."

Flick drove us back to Waimea that afternoon with a thousand dollars more in pledge money and three rolls of hog wire in the back of the truck. I didn't speak a word the entire drive home.

———

Much later while I was in college on the mainland I related the story to a classmate, my girlfriend at the time, and a psychology major.

"Hard Sell to Closing 101," I said grimly, totally oblivious at first that she saw only humor in the situation. "It wasn't funny at all growing up with that," I said. "It was coursework in human hardness and deceit. Dad wrote the book on it."

"Bullshit," she said. "Your father's the last of an unusual line of men, that's all."

When I appeared shocked, which I was, she shrugged. "Well, he is. He's just who he is, too. Nothing deep and dark about all of that, Josh, much as you'd like to make out otherwise. Frankly, I think he sounds wonderful. He sounds vital, alive."

Actually, I considered that to be part of the problem: my father was too much alive. I often wondered if the years would make him mellow, but somehow I doubted it.

"He was hard, real hard on my mother," I said.

"Physically? What do you mean?"

"Well, no, he never hit her or anything," I said, trailing off. He'd never been abusive in any true sense of the word, but he'd never been there for her in any certain way she needed either.

My girlfriend stood there watching me, assessing all that I had been saying, and not saying, too. "Hell, guess you had to be there." I couldn't believe that she was on my father's side. I never could figure it out, but women just liked my father.

"I bet he's so hard on himself it would knock you to your knees to know it," she said. "Haven't you read anything lately? Heard about the grieving of the American male?"

No. I had not. None outside of my own anyway.

"Look, Josh, I know you hate it when I go on like this, but part of this is a game for you and it's not a very happy game. If I were you, I'd let it go, move on with my life."

I never dated her again after that.

---

For known at least to the two of us, Flick and I had never seen eye to eye on anything, especially the furthering of my education after high school.

I went on and majored in English, pacifying my father with the idea that it might lead into law. Then one summer I came home to see Flick, planning to ask if he'd help fund my way to getting a masters in fine arts. Watercolor was my medium for expression; it was an aptitude and attitude I'd inherited from my mother. I hoped to make my living eventually as an artist, but in the meantime, I could teach.

Dad saw otherwise.

The moment he told me he wouldn't help fund anything outside of business or law, I knew the time had come for me to leave Hawaii. Mom's dying hadn't made my father and I any closer, so I saw no point in staying on.

Dad insisted on his own way, hoping to change my mind right up to the very moment I stepped out of his truck at the airport, claiming the rest of my life as my own.

"You've got a degree now, college boy, but that doesn't make you Michaelangelo or close to it. You're wasting your time going any further with this art crap. Come into the real world, work for me for awhile. That way if - "

I cut his sentence short with a look.

"Damn it, Josh! You have any idea what you're turning down? Do you know what some of the company's sons and daughters would give to have the chance I'm offering you?"

"Give it to one of them then. I don't want it. Just how many hotels can you put on this island anyway, Dad? Or does it even matter to you outside of the counting?"

I'd had enough of my father to last me three lives, his endless need to win. He always won too, often at the expense of people less shrewd than him. People like my mother. I'd vowed long ago not to make the same mistakes that she had made.

After she died, there had been a constant flow of new women in Flick's life, something I found hard to take. But it wasn't long before he seemed to settle on one. She was a young Japanese woman, quiet and easy to look at, firm with my father in a way I had never known anyone to be with him.

I liked her. Until I remembered where it was I had seen her before. Before Mom was known to be sick.

"Damn you! This is it. I'm through handing you things, making life easy for you. No more chances from me boy. I'm through."

"Great, Dad. Leaves me feeling complete, if you can even understand that," I said.

"You? Complete? Ha! You've never completed a damn thing in your life and now you feel complete?"

We drove the rest of the way to the Keahole Airport in silence, horses for some strange reason, foremost on my mind. My father raised champion quarter horses as his number one passion outside of work and winning big, just as his own father had done in Oklahoma. He tried to get me to ride with him and his new Japanese companion, but I refused. It was one more impossible connection between him and his only child.

Like my mother, I was scared to death of horses.

At the airport he grimly piled my bags onto the sidewalk, reaching into a back pocket of his jeans for his wallet. "Here," he said, thrusting several hundred dollar bills at me.

I shook my head. "Keep it, Dad. No more nuttin'," I said, imitating his Oklahoma twang, fully expecting to land on the sidewalk beside my own luggage.

"Take it, damn it," he insisted. "It's colder than a witch's tit back there on the mainland, especially the Oregon coast."

My mind played back an immediate image, a visual recording of Dad's choice of words.

"What's so damn funny?" Flick leaned in through the window of the truck to grab a pack of Camels off the dashboard.

I ignored his question and studied the man before me. This hard-driving father of mine, one of the biggest and most successful developers in the Hawaiian Islands, equating mainland winters with witch's tits. The definitive Malboro Man, my father, J.J. Flick. "What are you doing here anyway, Dad? I mean, really, what are you all about?"

Flick turned on the heel of his boot and kicked a front tire of the truck.

"Christ, Dad!" I said, jumping back a little. "Give it up." It was obvious to me how he felt. I was no blood connection that he could recognize, but I didn't exactly see mirror images of myself in him either.

"Making one hell of a lot of money, that's what I'm doing. How the heck do you think you ever got through Punahou? Nobody hands out scholarships to scrawny bodies like yours. It's first on the scrimmage line, Josh, not last."

I knew he'd drag it out for as long as he could, so taking hold of my bags I flashed him the high sign and walked away. I never did look back. Not once.

⸻

Now here I was years later with a letter in front of me, a letter from Flick. It was unlike any letter I'd ever received from him in the past. Nothing like the one announcing his marriage to the Japanese woman, a marriage I'd refused to attend or even acknowledge with a congratulatory card. It was nothing like the letters which came for a while afterwards either, until finally he stopped writing altogether.

This letter was different. Written on a single letterhead with J.J. Flick and Company stamped across the top. A letter dropped casually into my life like some child's paper airplane, yet with all the impact of a kamikaze pilot. My old girlfriend had been right after all. I had been playing a game, a very unhappy game.

The letter raised two new questions: how do you make up for a lifetime of alienation from someone you've only just realized you love more than anyone else in the world?

And who the hell was Alex Kimura?

⸻

## Alex

It's like this: no one ever gave me a wild baby pig before. No one ever gave me much of anything outside of Flick and my mother. When Flick put that pig in my arms, it was small as a kitten, only cuter, with skin soft as a human baby. Hoku was what I named him, the Hawaiian word for star.

I dressed Hoku in a little blue nightie I had saved from years ago and a doll named Binky. He'd trot behind me in that baby doll's nightgown, and I'd tie it in a knot on his backside to keep it from dragging in the dirt at the stables.

"Don't you go getting attached to that pig now, Alex," said Flick. "He's going to get big like all pigs do, and I expect he'll turn mean on you."

I picked up Hoku and held him close against my chest, deciding not to take Flick's remark seriously. That man often worried about the most unlikely things.

"I'm not kidding," said Flick. "Wild things often turn mean on you, but we'll be sure to find you a baby goat before that happens."

I hugged Hoku close, pulling his gown up snug around one shoulder, feeling it best to ignore Flick altogether. "Pig, pig, my little pig. Hoku, Hoku, hele on home to me." This was my way of telling the pig not to concern himself with Flick's gruff tone.

"He's cute now, Al, but he will grow up to be big," insisted Flick. "And mean."

I continued to ignore Flick.

"Alex!"

Hoku jumped in my arms, and snuggled so close to my belly it was as if he was trying to crawl inside to get born all over again. "Not this pig," I said. "He's mine and I'll keep him gentle forever. But I'll take that baby goat, too, if you don't mind."

Flick laughed so hard he went into another one of those coughing spasms, the kind that left him shaking afterwards. I didn't know what was so funny, but I loved it when he laughed.

I untied the knot in Hoku's nightgown, slipping it off his small clean body. Flick raised his eyebrows. "He follows me into his stalls at cleaning time and the gown will get all dirty if I leave it on," I explained.

Flick laughed harder than ever, coughing harder than ever, too. "Alex, you're worth a fortune, baby doll." He walked away laughing and coughing, shaking one hand out to his side in a half wave. "Got to get back to the office."

I wasn't sure how much I might be worth, but I could hear the sounds of happy long after he was out of sight.

———

Once, when I was saddling up Island Tales, Flick's quarter horse stud, there was an accident. Tales was being goofy – he kept swishing his tail from side to side, stamping the ground with his hooves. He stomped right down on Hoku. My pig squealed louder than a hurt child, scaring me as if he were my own baby, too.

I scooped him up and placed him gently on a bale of hay and immediately turned to Tales, and then I put that blasted horse back into his stall, the saddle leathers slapping against his sides as he danced round and round. When I picked up Hoku again, he was quiet as sleep. I ran up to the house as fast as I could go, doing my best not to jar the little pig. No one was there, so I ran all the way into town.

Dr. Buckley, a veterinarian, told me that Hoku couldn't be helped, that he was in too much pain to leave alone. The moment I realized what he really meant, I grabbed my pig and headed for the door. "Of course he's in pain. You would be too if a big studhorse had stomped down on your leg!"

I left that place faster than I had arrived and called the only person I could depend on. I called Flick.

"Whoa now, Alex. Where are you?" he asked.

"Corner of Wai'aka and Parker," I managed to get out.

"Stop crying, we'll fix that pig. You at that phone booth outside Osaya's Liquors?"

I nodded my head as if Flick could see me. "Stay put. I'll be right there," he said.

Five minutes later he was, just like that.

We drove out to Tai Hanohano's house, way out Mana Road side. Tai worked for Parker Ranch as a paniolo for more than sixty years and he's the oldest person I know still walking upright after that many years and miles in a saddle. Tai never talks much, he just listens real close. Sometimes he bobs his head in a peculiar way, growling down low from his chest. Flick says that means he's feeling with you, thinking past what anyone could with mere words. Flick says that whenever Tai is doing any kind of healing work it's best to let him growl for as long as he needs to growl.

Tai lived in a tiny one-room ranch shack with two windows and no furniture outside of a single table made of old scrap lumber bleached white as bone from the Hawaiian sun. A single dwarf sized tree sat off to one side of the table. Tai placed the tree on the floor, talking to it the entire time.

"Bonsai," whispered Flick to me as the old man took Hoku from my arms and placed him on the table where the plant had been. "That's one of his prize trees right there. Tai's famous for his bonsai. And his healing," he added when I tugged down hard on his hand.

The Chinese-Hawaiian man grunted as he looked over Hoku; he growled deep down in his chest twice. My pig must have known that Tai would make him well again because he didn't budge an inch. Tai grunted once more and nodded at Flick. Flick squeezed my shoulder but he kept his eyes on the old man.

Hoku whimpered one time, human-like and scared. I shut my eyes tight, and when next I peeked, there snug around Hoku's right leg was a pretty white bandage. Flick whistled his admiration. "What did you use for a splint, Tai man?"

"Green branch of the kiawe tree. The wood is strong, gentle. Like a good mother."

The old man motioned us outside, a finger pressed to his lips. "Sssh, pig sleep good now. You leave him here with me overnight. Bimeby you come back for get him in the morning, dat's best thing."

We set Hoku free in the hills of North Kohala where Flick and I loved to ride, a few months after Hoku's leg had healed. Flick told me that my pig would find other wild pigs like himself in those hills; we cheered, raising our hands high in salute as Hoku trotted off into the wilds of his new home.

Mother was a Kimura and I am, too. "Don't ever forget that you are a Kimura, Alex," she told me.

"Like hell she is, she's a Flick!" my father would roar in return. Then he'd shake his head, and seem to think it over. "But it's not really the name, it's what you learn from having the name. No, it's not that either. It's beyond that. Heck, it's all a mystery when you get right down to it. Least I'm coming to see it that way."

Sometimes his words and philosophy confused me, but his stories never did. The story he told me most often was this one about a sand crab.

There were once two crabs who lived on a sandy white beach. One crab was young and bold, the other ancient and slow with barnacles on his back from knowing the sea and shore for a very long time.

One day the younger crab became angry during a defensive arts class that all crabs were required to take, and he told his teacher, "This is silly! Dancing sideways, dancing backwards, always being attacked from the front and scurrying off, prideless and gutless. I will never do that when I am confronted by my enemy. I shall stand my ground and snatch him up with my claws and never, never let him get away!"

The old crab was concerned for the young crab. "You are young and foolish, small one. I am weary of working with someone who wishes not to learn. The Wise One lives in the rock farthest from the other rocks. Go and seek his counsel before it is too late for you." And with these last words, the teacher slowly backed off from the young crab.

"What a goofy old crab," said the little crab. "What does he know anyway?" But feeling uneasy, and curious as well, he decided to go and find the Wise One, the oldest and most knowledgeable crab of them all.

He found the Wise One alone in his Rock Cave painting exquisite pictures of sea anemones and small fish swimming in an ocean of soft blues and greens. In the background of the painting were many crabs dancing in a swirling array of color and current upon the wall of the ocean cave.

"How beautiful," said the little crab. "I would like to do that." But looking down at his small left claw and his only slightly larger right one, he shook his head sadly. "My claws are too small to create anything as wonderful as that, Wise One. How did yours grow to be so big and strong? How can anyone like me even dream of painting pictures like those?"

The Wise One smiled and painted a single line of indigo blue onto the wall with his left claw, following it with a brilliant splash of violet with the other. Then bowing, as if beginning a slow dance, both claws waving in the air, he turned towards the little crab. "By dancing sideways, and dancing backwards. For that is the way of the Sand Crab. Therein lies his true power. And by using these," he said, touching the little crab gently with a mighty claw, "for creating, not destroying."

When Flick was finished with the story, my mother would always say, "Listen, Alex. People fail to listen and so they miss the secret. Much of the world is like that little crab, they think the power is in the claw. But the secret lies not in the fight. The secret – and you must listen with your eyes open, child – lies in the dance. Watch. Listen. And you just might discover the secret."

"Yeah, kid," Flick would say. "Keep your nostrils flared and your eyeballs peeled."

———

The morning that Flick came down to the stables I knew he was there before I saw him because of the smell of his tobacco. He stood there tall to me, his dark hair streaked by years in the sun. For the first time I noticed the splashes of gray around his face and eyes. To me he looked so handsome, as if he was going somewhere special.

"Alex!" He seemed especially happy to see me that morning. It was almost as if he had forgotten that here was where I was supposed to be. But what he said next scared me more than anything ever has again.

"Came down to see our champion horse, Alex. I came down to check up on the greatest mare of all, our girl Light Image here."

He reached up to pat Tale's neck and the big studhorse snorted nervously, pawing the dirt up from the ground, getting dust all over Flick's nice suit. "Great mare, this old gal. Your mother's favorite, too. Saddle her up and the three of us will go for a mountain ride this afternoon, ok?" He winked at me and turned back the other way, and was gone before I could say a word.

I looked up towards the feed area where the hay was stacked. A small pile of tobacco had spilled out onto one of the bales like an angry bruise, dark and ominous against the goldness of the hay. Flick's pipe lay tipped to one side next to the tobacco.

That's when I knew that something was wrong with Flick. He never left behind his pipe, only the smell of his tobacco.

And both my mother and Light Image had died more than three years ago.

⸺

## Josh

The long, cool form of a man lay as if dead on an efficiently designed recovery room table. The design of the table was hopeful, its purpose to deliver and retrieve persons going into or coming out of surgery. Hopeful yet still metallic, still indifferent.

My departure that morning at the airport was far from where I found myself now, walking alongside my father, feeling hopelessly out of place. Moving out of a nurse's way I watched as two white coated individuals navigated my father's table at an angle towards the bed docked in the middle of the room. Never speaking, barely making eye contact, they lifted the patient in one clean movement onto sheets stretched taut as sails, then anchored the I.V. bottles and lines to the hospital bed railings.

Running one last look over my father, they nodded silently at me and left, their exit as efficient as their charts.

I was alone with my father. "Flick? Dad. How's it going? I got here as soon as I could."

My father's still form moved slightly and seemed to twitch involuntarily. His eyelids fluttered open, only to close again. He sighed. The eyelids fluttered once more, remaining open. A soft flash of an expression, a yawn maybe, passed over my father's face, lighting like the whisper of a butterfly. His mouth opened slowly, a grimace of pain shot across his face.

"Don't talk yet, Dad." I kneeled down beside him. "Ssssh, hush, Dad. Don't try to talk."

The grimace turned into a smile. "Anything to drink around here? I could use one straight up right now – you know how much I hate hospital food, Josh."

"I don't know whether I can find you a drink here, but I'll do anything to find you some decent clothes. Never seen anyone look quite like you do in a hospital gown, Dad."

Flick began to laugh, but his body warned him not to.

"God, Dad, I'm so —"

Flick reached up and took a handful of my hair. "Ssh: don't you say it. Don't you dare say it. Ever tell you about the first time my daddy put me on a horse?"

His hand had slipped down to my chin; he cupped it briefly like my mother would have, his hand only slipping away after I'd shook my head. "No." I barely got the word out.

His eyes closed for a moment; he smiled up at the ceiling. "Helen Keller," he mumbled.

"Dad? What does she have to do with getting on a horse?"

"Nothing really, she just came to mind for a second there. There's more than one way of being blind I guess." He adjusted himself slightly on the bed; I moved closer, too. When he spoke again it was barely above a whisper, but I heard him on every level that there was to hear on.

"My father first put me on a horse when I was five years old. It was a pony actually, but it might as well have been a Brontosaurus – I was that scared. Well, he swung me on up there and then slapped that pony on the ass and off it went, me and that pony racing around the arena like together we made up a whole new animal. My mother was a real lady, but that day she became a crazy thing. She screamed and carried on at my father something fierce. I think I might have been ok after the third or fourth time around if she hadn't carried on so – you know how kids are. Fall down, never even think of crying till some adult asks if they've been hurt ... Anyway, something changed between my mother and father from that day forth and I always thought it was my fault."

He sounded as if he were in pain again. Yet it was another kind of pain, the kind I understood all too well. But never in a million years would I have pictured it on him.

"It wasn't your fault, Dad," I said.

"I know that. That is, I know it up here," he said, reaching up a hand to touch his head like he was tipping an invisible hat at me. His hand fell back onto the bed. I covered it with my own and never moved it again till I left the hospital later that evening.

"Ok now. You remember the first time I put you on a horse?"

I had tried hard all my life to forget such a time. But I nodded.

"People you think are your closest friends and strongest allies will turn on you sometimes. All I'd wanted to do at the time was give you a lesson in prudence," he said.

"It turned into a lesson about trust, Dad!" I objected.

"Hear me out, ok? Prudence. At the time I had lost a quarter of a million dollars when my net worth was less than seventy thousand. Jake Albright was responsible – hell, I was responsible, I know that. But Jake was the one got me to invest what cash I had at the time. Only as it turned out, Jake knew that the project was doomed, that it would fail and take us all right down with it. He had that much of an inside view of the whole thing as it turned out. As usual, he was out to make his own ass look special to those damn fool friends of his."

"Jake? Jake Albright? You grew up with him – he was your best friend. You played handball with the man for years!" I said, stunned.

"Still do play handball with him. He's a great opponent on the court, too. But I never have nor will I ever again do business with him. Further more, I'm rich now and he's not and he still can't figure out that part of the story."

"I don't get it," I said, and I didn't. I wasn't making the connection at all. When I was eleven years old, my father decided it was time for me to graduate from riding my pony and go to riding real horses. I was always small for my age, so Flick held the big bay mare by the reins to keep her still while I climbed on. Just as my leg was swinging up and over her back, and I was about to settle into the saddle, my own father booted the mare in the belly with his knee. The mare jumped sideways. I lost my balance and landed not in the saddle, but in the dust on the other side of the spooked mare.

"Don't ever trust anyone that much," my father had said. "Not even me."

My father looked down at my hand on his upon the bed and up at me again. "Pretty screwy thing to do to a kid, wasn't it?"

I bit down hard on the inside of my cheek but it didn't do any good.

"Glad you can finally laugh about it. I doubt I ever will," said Flick. "I figured out real quick how to make a million bucks but damned if I ever figured out how to do the right thing by small boys. I've been a sonofabitch my whole damn life when it comes to you. I want to tell you that I'm a —"

"Don't say it, don't you dare say it. Besides, I'm an idiot."

"Na, you're no idiot. You're just hardheaded. Good thing too. I had no idea that mare could move fast as she did, she was always such a slug on cattle."

---

## The Hill

Horse and rider climbed a rocky, twisted path imprinted into a lasting-ness by so many cattle for so many years. A short distance from the top, the horse began an easy lope, scaling the summit of the trail and continuing the journey back down again in a safer fashion.

The horse's shoulders moved freely with the well-muscled tact of a dancer. The rider's movements matched those of the horse, the wind-swept plains of lower Waikoloa their only stage, the fierce winds and thistles their only audience.

Approaching the base of a monumental hill, the girl took a firmer hold of her mount and deepened her seat, gathering the horse with her legs in a warning cue. The horse danced sideways, flexing at the poll, anticipating his rider's next commands. Backing the animal up in four light steps, the girl lowered her hands and felt the answering propulsion of the horse he had named Island Tales beneath her as the equine athlete leaped into a full gallop cast upon the hill.

Gaining power with every stride the horse ran as if to use himself up in a single headlong rush. One more burst of strength and the horse moved sharply to the left, jumping over a dry ravine and moving upwards along the trail.

Trusting her horse's sense of direction, the rider held onto the fork of the saddle and, closing her eyes, gave in to the feeling of the horse and the hill.

At the top of the small mountain she looked out on an expanse of island that was her world. Far to the right lay the green hills of North Kohala, the birthplace of Hawaiian kings. To the left Waikoloa's rugged landscape opened arms all the way down to the sea, then seemed to go on forever, undetected by human eyes.

"Come on, Tales. I know what I'm going to do now. Let's go home to Flick."

---

### Josh

The knoll outside my father's house was always a favorite spot for me as a boy with an active imagination and no brothers or sisters to share my dreams with. By closing my eyes I could envision soldiers in the desert, their wide white robes billowing, their steeds draped in braided gold spliced with jewels that glistened in the sweat of the desert heat and sun. I could actually hear the horses's steel bits clanking, see the saliva dripping from the horses's mouths, their Arabian hooves dancing across the sandy floor.

But the day my father lived forever was beyond anyone's imagination.

I was eating lychee, peeling the skin to get to the fruit beneath, sucking up the sweetness before it could burst free to my shirt. Then, closing my eyes like I did as a child when trying to see the something that only I could see, I opened them back up again – and immediately dropped the small red balls of fruit.

For there coming across the Waikoloa plains was a horse and two riders, and as they rode closer I knew exactly who they were: Alex and my father.

One child emerging woman, and one sick and dying man, riding across the harshness of Waikoloa on the horse my father named Island Tales.

As they approached the last narrow, rocky path leading directly to the stables, I hurried down to greet them.

Tales stopped right in front of me, shoving me backwards with his nose. My first impulse was to hug the big animal, the first time I'd felt like hugging a horse in my life.

"See? You've got horse sense whether you like it or not," said Flick. "Well, here we all are – nothing like a family reunion."

Alex watched me shyly from her perch on top of Tales, my father's arms wrapped about her waist. She smiled, her face trembling, her eyes bright and wet. "Hi, Josh," she said, reaching down to squeeze my shoulder gently. "I'm Alex."

"I know." And I touched my sister back.

# THE CACTUS

When he was alive, the man I learned later was my grandfather – though I knew him then as the Cactus – told me stories. They were small stories, horse operas, apologues he made authentic with his own voice, whether or not they were his to begin with.

The one he told me most often I later referred to as his calculated favorite. Favorite, because he told it brand new with each telling; calculated, because I sensed he had a purpose in mind with the telling. Which was more than likely so with anything he told me, but it was this story only that left me uneasy and tense in the body. It was this story only that made my throat swell with a knowledge I couldn't push aside as it rubbed up soft and much too close to something I didn't have a word for yet.

He called it the Creation Story, and since he was the ruling adult, and I but a small child, I chose to listen each time he told it. I guess you might think I could have shut my ears or turned my attention somewhere else, but you'd be wrong. No one could shut their ears when the Cactus spoke, though there was a place or two where I interrupted.

"Listen up, Arlin, when God brings you into this world, He does so by His very breath. Holding you in the palm of one mighty hand, He blows gently, yet with the strength of a hurricane, right on top your little baby head till you curl into a birth ball and burst through the heavens on your way to …"

"God blows you off his hand and out of the sky?" I asked. The image was a bit too incredible. Even for me. The Cactus was forever telling me stories that stretched my imagination – along with my patience. I also knew he had plans for my future, plans which included my becoming the first woman minister and spiritual healer in our family. I wanted no part of any of it, for I was determined to be the best dog and pony trainer in all of circus history, and if God was on my side about that, well then, we could be colleagues of a sort anyway. But as for preaching God's message, let's just say I had a few messages of my own to get out first.

*65*

"Are you telling me that God actually blew some small child … a baby … out of the sky? And straight off his hand?" To me, the idea was downright mean.

The Cactus, the name given to my grandfather by who only knows – God Himself maybe – calmly removed his reading glasses and polished them with the tail of his red flannel shirt. A gesture he used to stall for time only, as he'd just cleaned them moments before. He drummed his fingers on the arm of his favorite reading chair, an old willow rocker, and waited. Waited till I couldn't stand it any more.

I scowled down at my boots, kicking at the sides of the old pine bench I was sitting on, and rolled my eyes at him. He took that as his cue to read again and moved his glasses back up on his nose. "Where was I now?" he asked.

"God's blowing that baby out of the sky," I said, pretending not to notice his amused expression. "I never told you I didn't like your story. I simply find it a bit … unplausible."

"Implausible."

"Whatever."

Crossing my arms, I stared straight ahead like I'd watched Billy Lee do with strangers from out of town when they got to asking too many questions. Billy Lee can tune out his own mother if he cares to, a feat I find remarkable, but a feat I never had the chance of trying on since my mother beat me and everyone else to it by tuning out the whole planet first and forever. But as for tuning out my grandfather, I doubt even Billy Lee could pull that off.

"The bible doesn't know everything there is to know about God, I guess." I kicked one two, one two, on that old pine bench, coming down hard on the count of two.

"Shall I resume?" he asked, his eyebrows raised so high I thought his glasses would flip right off his face.

"Resume," and I leaned into his story, bracing my back against that slab of pine.

"And He held the baby lightly in one palm, His eyes soft as summer clouds on a kind day, yet more tempestuous than the fiercest wind, and He spoke to that child: Go! And always do it your way, for that is how it has been willed. Just as you have had your birth – buttass first in order to see best the world you're coming and going from, so you shall have your life and …"

"Like me, isn't that so, Cactus? That baby could've been me." Though I'd heard the story before, it never failed to thrill me.

It wasn't till years later I learned that baby was me, and like God Himself my grandfather had certain ideas in mind he wanted me to accomplish. That story was just one of his ways of planting the seeds of who he wanted me to become. Or maybe it was his way of pruning back the branches of what he already feared me to be, and for years after he died I swear I could feel him reaching up from the dirt to tug at my feet like they were roots at his fingertips; I felt him blow soft on all the new leaves I sprouted. And twice I knew it could have been no other who sent the winds of fury followed quick as lightning, by even fiercer embraces of salvation in the form of gentle hugs and words from total strangers. He had that much power over me as a small child and well on after that. He shook my guts up. He presented me with the brazen idea that I could grow towards the sky and earth at the same time. Of course, none of this I realized till I was grown. None of this I understood till I had moved past the pain of knowing I was the last one left in our family. And before I found out I wasn't the last.

But I have to tell you this part of the story first. For the Creation Story was my grandfather's way of easing the worries of my family. It smoothed over our common pain. Ours was a family short on attention and long on superstition. Superstition they paid close attention to. Why, if you were a complete unknown and just so happened to mention you heard voices from out of nowhere – for one example – they would have you sitting at the next family meal like you were part of them. There was even a time or two when my family had such strangers convinced that they were one of us.

But fortunately my grandfather made distinctions between real family and outsiders, and managed to find those temporary members gas money, train tickets, or a hand-drawn map for those strong enough to leave town on foot. He found them whatever it was they needed to get back on their way. The fact was and still is that, unlike the wanderers who slipped in and out of our family's lives, prodding and poking us in directions not intended by the Cactus, most of us never managed to find our way anywhere.

My grandfather moved his glasses back down on his nose and studied me like I was a confusing piece of information altogether. And that I can be, I know. He cocked his head patiently to one side, fingers drumming on the arms of his rocking chair.

"Come to think on it, you were born butt first now, weren't you?"

I nodded proudly.

He peered at a point above my nose and stared so intently, I reached up and brushed away whatever it was might be there: a speck of dust maybe, smudged dirt from wiping my face with a dusty shirt sleeve after riding my horse. Or maybe … chocolate. I was fond of chocolate. Then he scratched his chin and leaned way forward, close into my face. "That's it, that's gotta' be it. That's the reason why you butt in often as you do. Funny how I never caught onto that being the reason why before."

He gave my knee a thump and a shake, and I vowed silence for the remainder of the story, only the backs of my boots drumming one two, one two, on that bench.

"And balancing both head and heart, Spirit Child, for even a tiny baby knows straight off that this life is All Life, thus God made this declaration: As it is with all my creations, in this life you are destined to do one great thing and one great thing only. Yet when it is done it shall be said, indeed it shall be sung and wrote about … that it was …" Here he'd pause and give me a look before continuing "… it was the greatest thing of all."

This part always shook me up. I was left without a clue as to what to say, or even less, what to feel. It was like a tornado had rushed by my bones and whisked them clean, leaving my head emptier than a hole without a fence post. The small but very sweet comfort I received from the swinging of my boots seemed to stop of its own accord, and I felt entirely abandoned by this point, this turn in the story. For I sensed that something way bigger than me was expected by the Cactus: something bold and generous, something beyond me. Something so clean and fine it would have to be pulled out of my soul with tweezers, one sliver at a time. It wouldn't come easy – I knew that much to the soles of my heels clad in hard leather.

But most of all, I knew it was a horrible mistake to expect such goodness out of me.

For even if there was a God, then both God and I would have to agree I wasn't designed to be that kind of good. I wasn't designed to be that kind of brave, or that kind of tender either. I wasn't designed to be any one of those things my grandfather lived to breathe about to anyone who would listen to the telling of his story.

And since I doubted the Cactus's belief that there was one solitary omniscient somebody watching out for everyone and everything – to me the very idea was a ridiculous exercise in ego for any one Being to attempt alone – a part of me reserved the right to hold tight to as much indignation as I could muster, that the Cactus would ever dream of something so big coming out of me.

Besides, I knew the Cactus wasn't exactly that kind of good either.

Yet indignation was never fire enough to break the spell of my grandfather. It was just a smoke screen, a futile attempt on my part at another point of view. A point of view I wasn't too sure of anyway.

All of me was drum silent. Even the pounding of my heart was soft as the step of a garden sparrow; it fluttered up against my rib cage, looking, listening, for the rest of the story that was hiding there. Frustrating as that was, all of me did feel sort of holy and open to seeing almost anything. God maybe. And if He – or She – had appeared right then and there, I doubt I'd have been too surprised. In fact, the presence of a third party might have eased the tension between me and my grandfather.

The Cactus would pause at this place in the story to watch me (not that I let on I knew he was watching me) and then go on with the telling.

"And then the Great Spirit Father said: Go now, go into the world, Spirit Child, and become of body. Go! Don't fret ever. For poets dream of one great poem and painters dream of one great painting. You are the Poem. You are the Painting. Indeed, you are my Work, so go, and it shall find you.

And then the Spirit Father blew His breath gently on the palm of one mighty hand, bringing forth the winds from within and spilling them onto the spirit baby curled pure as gold, nestled there sweet in the hand of God. The baby rolled over, tucking tiny feet to tiny hands and she giggled, unfolding and rolling over once more, her whispering limbs waving in the air like the eyelashes of angels."

The Cactus paused for a moment, then closing his eyes he drew a deep breath and went on.

"God blew slow and strong once more, His breath directed towards the west, and the spirit baby was gone from the heavens. Only the sounds of laughter remained, laughter echoing, crashing the stillness of clouds like waves upon a shore. The laughter broke down upon the beaches, breaking down sand into more sand, sweeping back driftwood and broken shells and embracing it all back again, for these things were most important. These things were not what they appeared to be at all. These things were what He used to make the world up all over again. These things …"

And of course I knew what "these things" were, though each time I heard it, I could scarcely believe it.

"… these things are the building blocks of God: the bones of angels left behind."

We sat and faced each other at the end of the telling, both quiet but thinking loud and hard nonetheless.

"The bones of angels belong to you, child." He must have told me this a million times if he told he once, and each time a chill would play up my spine all the way to my teeth and back down again, catching firm in the small of my back. But I'd shrug it off. I couldn't figure. For I was confused by a small child's thoughts then, or maybe, a small child's fears. I felt things and I listened soft and close, but I didn't know; I didn't understand.

And to save my life I couldn't stop thinking how that baby was blown out of the sky like that! Though it felt safe enough the way my grandfather told it, I guess. I kind of liked the idea. But one thing kept rolling around in my head like a giant marble with no score in sight.

"Now how can that be, Cactus? Do angels even have bones?"

My grandfather took off his reading glasses, leaned way back in his chair and laugh-roared like the mountain lion of a man he was, nearly startling me – a small bird of a child – right off that pine bench. And I grinned back, laughing with the lion, though I didn't know what the joke was about.

But I think I knew then just how that spirit baby felt and as I closed my eyes I rolled that small piece of life around in my head to the sounds of my grandfather's laughter. What I did was try hard to make a picture in my mind as to what God looked like.

But all I saw was a face scarred by fire and too much pain, too many hard-working years without a payback. Still, it was a face that shined and smiled and spoke to me like no face ever has again. All I saw was the face of my grandfather.

So when he walked back into my life like he wasn't the ghost he was, and when I saw I wasn't the only one who could see him, this ghost, this man come back from the dead, I knew that the time had come for me to be who he'd always known I could be. Who he'd always known deep down I wanted to be.

But it sure the hell didn't make it any easier.

# THE LOSING OF THESE THINGS

The first inclination Hank had that Este might be a few sandwiches short of a picnic was when she asked him to build her a tree house in the front yard. Like the weeds he swore weren't there a day earlier, she appeared suddenly in front of him with her request. "I'd sure like it if you built me a tree house out front," she said.

Hank stood up from his yard work, wiped his forehead with a shirt sleeve, wiggled his shoulders back and forth a little. It was his way of shifting gears. There was no mistaking what he had heard. Hank knew this much by Este's stance. She stood there, arms across her chest, the familiar barricade she put up against any hint of resistance. Hank thought it best not to offer any either. He wiggled his shoulders again, took a deep breath, held it. He held his breath till the craving for a cigarette, which still presented itself at moments such as these, disappeared. "Well, now Este, why the front yard?"

He asked this question with the well-masked resolve of a man who has lived with a woman long enough to know better than to ask the obvious: have you lost your mind completely? That, and knowing from experience that saying anything only helped to stall – never stop – the inevitable. Este was as persistent as she was direct. Still, it irked him that he even had to ask. Given a choice, he'd prefer that the request of a tree house by a fifty-two year old woman and grandmother not be made at all.

"Este? Why the front? Why not out back? Out back's more private."

Hank gave his wife a long look before settling back down on his knees in the dirt where he'd been uprooting the bamboo growing alongside the house. Fire hazard, bamboo. Much as he liked the proliferation of growth that had taken root like a miniature Polynesian jungle at the far west side of their home, this was not Hawaii or close to it. The bamboo had to go due to its preference for nestling in like a second skin where the warmth of the old house provided also, a wind break. Bamboo bunched together like thieves, and no matter how hard he tried to retrain it towards some degree of independence, it insisted on ganging up where it could do the most harm. Hank knew these things, he was the chief of the all-volunteer fire department in town, yet he was fond of the bamboo and wished it would heed his coaxing towards a separate life a little further from the house. Seemed everything had a mind of its own these days, including vegetation. Still, he had to stay on top of things (he was king of this jungle, wasn't he?), and that meant bamboo or anything else zeroing in too close for comfort to his family's home.

"There's more trees to choose from in the backyard, Este."

"Of course there's more trees … but I just need one. I don't want to be out back any more, Hank, I want to be out in front. I've been out back my whole life." Then, waving one hand out to the side of her face as if dismissing both Hank and the subject of tree-houses altogether, Este was gone as quick as she had shown up.

Hank stayed put on his knees, looking off in the direction his wife had taken. Este was a force of nature to be reckoned with, and Hank had chosen long ago to be a part of that nature. He clasped his hands together in his lap and closed his eyes as if in prayer. He was as quiet as the proverbial still water. Though his eyes were closed, inside his head they were like two wild things fluttering up against the skin of their lids. He waited for the familiar upheaval to present itself in his mind – swirling lights, too many pictures, most of them overlapping; sporadic and out of sync like the damn cable that was forever going out on his T.V. But Hank was a patient man and he kept his eyes closed. He didn't open them again till he was sure that the picture coming into focus in his mind was the one he would put to paper in pen and ink.

Time – and maybe an argument or two with Este on the overall design – was all there was between him and a tree house. All right already, in the damn front yard for Pete's sakes.

---

Este had just decided she was in love with her husband again, when Heidi walked down Hemlock Street in her wet suit causing Hank to go all goo-goo eyed and act more a fool than he usually did when a young and beautiful woman made a spectacle of herself.

Which Este said in so many words.

Hank took his eyes off Heidi long enough to keep from hitting a small dog that was crossing the street. The terrier-looking dog was hellbent in a linear direction for Heidi who ignored the animal as it caught up with her till it began to leap and scratch at her ankles, then Heidi swatted it on the head. The dog, though surprised, didn't seem to think Heidi's intentions were necessarily discouraging, and assaulted Heidi's ankles again. Heidi lunged forward – the exact same lunge that the instructor on the aerobics video insisted would give Este gluts like Heidi – and made a karate chop in the air so close to the dog's face it yelped and took off running. Then Heidi shook her long mane of sun-streaked hair and walked on down the street, her body taut and silent, only her stomach muscles rippling (or so Este imagined) beneath a sleek sea suit of neoprene rubber.

"What do you mean? She's not making a spectacle, she's making a statement."

Hank had made this last comment with pride, as if Heidi were related to them. Este gave Hank a sharp look and entertained the idea of thumping him one, snorting her disgust instead.

"She's a bully besides. That was old Mrs. Anderson's dog and that animal wouldn't hurt a fly."

"Nope, but then that dog's pestier than any damn fly. About the only thing it can't do is buzz your ear."

Este ignored this remark and put a hand on the steering wheel – Hank was still looking at Heidi with unabashed admiration. Although they weren't doing more than fifteen miles an hour, tourists did have a way of walking out in traffic during the summer season. It was as if they'd entered some new twist of a bumper car event at a carnival. Tempting though it was to wake them out of their dazed stupors, the police didn't look fondly on locals bumping tourists. A time or two though, Este had leaned on her horn with furious delight, making it her duty to turn a slow shuffle into a startled leap across the street.

Heidi was something else though. The girl didn't shuffle, she seemed to glide as if on ice. Este shook her head. "If that had been my dog now ..."

"Now that makes no sense at all, Este ... you'd never own a dog like that. The girl feels good about being alive's all. And hey, there's nothing like a good display of local color to bring a town together."

Hank made this remark as if even he knew this was stretching it. It wasn't that Este begrudged Hank a look at Heidi's display of a transplanted California girl's healthy physique. It wasn't that Este begrudged any vital man a look at Heidi. It was the fact that Heidi was not – try hard as she might to be – a local. Colorful? Yes. But local? This was Oregon after all and Oregonians were a conservative bunch for the most part, radical though they might be beneath the surface.

That the surface of Heidi's skin didn't reveal a single unsightly bulge or bump when clung to by neoprene and saltwater failed to enamor Este of the young woman's becoming an Oregonian even less. Heidi was neither conservative or radical. Heidi was simply flamboyant.

Which Este said in so many words.

"Aw, heck, Este. Give the girl a break, she's just having some fun. It's not like she'll look like that forever."

"Or feel like it either," Este mumbled.

Hank shot his wife a surprised look. "Well, see now? You do have a sense of these things after all. You do know."

Yeah. Este knew all right. Did she ever.

———

Hank and Este had met early one spring when Hank needed a young horse started under saddle. Hank had been sober for nearly a year – long enough to realize that the Quarter Horse filly he'd bought on impulse (an impulse fueled by several six-packs of Olympia beer) would no longer do his bidding.

"Heck, when I bought her, she followed me right into that fellow's trailer like a puppy," Hank said, waving a hand out to one side in disgust.

But it seemed to Este that the disgust was a mask, for Hank spoke with genuine concern, a touch of sadness even. Este sensed how once again an innocent animal had been hauled into someone's life to alleviate one of the predicaments of being human – in Hank's case, loneliness. Este said nothing and just watched the big solemn man who stood before her clasping and unclasping his hands. Like his horse he appeared, well, troubled.

"No kidding, you should have seen her," Hank added, his tone wistful yet proud. "She really was like a puppy dog. Used to follow me everywhere … used to follow me around the yard, out to the workshop. Hell, once, she even picked up a hammer and carried it over to me. It was like she was trying to figure out what it was I needed next. This may sound crazy, but it was like she wanted a job!"

Este's eyes got big and she raised her eyebrows slightly. It was her opinion that horses did need jobs. Although hammering nails wasn't a good match for a horse.

Hank, inspired by Este's attentions, continued.

"Heck, one time she followed me into the house all the way to the kitchen. I chased her back out of course. Yeah … she was like a little old puppy dog all right."

Este surmised that Hank didn't know much about puppies, and even less about horses.

"What do you think's the real reason why she followed you into all those places?"

Hank looked puzzled. "Hell, if I know for sure. I suspect – and I could be wrong, I'm no cowboy – but I always figured she came looking for me. She's kind of a social type, friendly and all. That's why I call her 'Babe.' She's a babe, she is. 'Course, I haven't paid much attention to her for over a year so she probably has some resentment over that. I took sick for a while …" Hank blushed bright red at this last remark "… then lost all track of time. Friend of mine who used to have horses as a kid helped me pasture her on some acreage he has. Today's the first chance I've had to play around with her again."

Hank pulled his hands out of his pockets and methodically cracked his knuckles, one at a time. When he finished he shook his hands in the air like they were wet and needed drying out. Then the rest of his body gave a little shudder, like it was one big knuckle trying to crack itself some relief. It was an unfamiliar movement to Este, but interesting all the same. She suspected it was a direct clue to Hank's state of mind.

"I don't suppose we did too good at it either," he said.

All it took was one look at Hank's torn clothes to figure out that much. Hank did look unhappy. And if it hadn't been for the fact that Este had more than her share of people with no horse sense trying to turn horses into puppies, she might have felt sorry for him. She managed to give Hank a grim smile. Hank smiled back.

"I found your name in the yellow pages. In your ad it said how you specialized in problem horses …" Hank ducked his head. "But she's not a problem, she just has some residual resentment going on's what I think."

Este studied Hank from the tips of his work boots to the slightly balding spot on his head, figuring it was there in the weather lined map of this man's face that she would find the source of his horse problem. She found it hard to keep from staring into his eyes (blue, Paul Newman blue). For some uneasy reason, her own senses were especially tuned in to this man's situation. She took note of this fact and vowed not to let it get the best of her. Business was business and working horses was Este's. For a split second she closed her eyes – Hank was saying something else now. The exact words failed to register on Este's brain, but it was how he said it that seemed important. Hank's tone was hopeful, but then hope was all he had left. That and a very spoiled and bored young horse that was anything but a puppy dog.

Este nodded at Hank, but her eyes were on the horse now. She lightly clapped her hands just as Babe was about to steal a bite out of Hank's shoulder. The filly jumped back, startled, and Hank moved towards her to console her.

"Don't do that!"

This time Hank jumped. Babe merely shifted her weight forward enough to land a hoof on Hank's tennis shoe, but was otherwise unperturbed. Hank swore lightly and the filly shifted her weight again, freeing his foot.

"She does that sometimes," he said by way of apology. "She doesn't mean any harm by it though."

"The hell she doesn't! She doesn't even recognize that she's a horse, for Christ's sakes. She thinks she's human."

Hank absolutely beamed at this remark and hired Este on the spot. Less than a year later Este's uneasy sense did get the best of her. She and Hank were married in a small and poignantly silly ceremony, all of it performed on horseback.

That had been over twenty years ago, and though Este figured that Hank had finally come to realize that horses were better off knowing they were horses, sometimes she wasn't sure. All Este knew was that when it came to humans, horses got by with a little bit of people sense. But it seemed like people got by with no sense at all.

⸺

Hank felt it wasn't that Este was off so much as she wasn't quite on either. The usual things not only failed to rile her, they blew on by altogether.

She had taken to watching reruns of old movies – Butch Cassidy and the Sundance Kid for one. Over and over and over again. When Hank heard her ask, "Who are those guys?" in harmony with Newman and Redford for what he swore was the hundredth time, he stormed into the living-room and demanded, "Who are what guys, goddamn it, who are what guys?"

Este's response was to shimmy down further into the pillowed fortress of Hank's easy chair, like she too was doing her best to hide from the Super Posse.

That Este refused to watch any film made in the last decade – hell, make that the last two decades – was all the more irksome to Hank.

"How about we watch one of those new releases, hon? You know, the ones they actually make in color?"

Butch and Sundance had just broken into Sheriff Bledsoe's office in the dead of night. "I'm too old to hunt up another job! You could at least have the decency to draw your guns!"

"C'mon Este, you must know all the lines yourself by now ... Este? You hear me?"

But it seemed Este only had eyes and ears for Butch and Sundance.

"There's something out there that scares you, huh?"

Hank shook his head. Maybe there was something out there that scared Butch and Sundance, but what was scaring Hank wasn't out there at all. It was all right here in the sanctity of his own house: hollowed down sadly in his favorite chair.

———

The second inclination Hank had that Este's state of mind might be questionable came around the time of the church raffle. Which became the Pony Project. Este's showing up in church at all, and taking June Day besides, should have been sign enough.

June Day was eighty-nine years old and determined to bail before she made ninety. If she made ninety, the whole town would be on her case to live to be a hundred and to hell with that. Who needed that kind of pressure?

Este and June were friends and "friends don't let friends drive them to church" was Este's motto. But she was making an exception in this case. June had refused to go anywhere for over a year since her husband died. So when June called Este about the raffle, Este enthusiastically agreed to drive her to Our Savior's Grace Lutheran Church. Hell, if that's what it would take to get her friend June out of the house again, Este would take her to church.

They arrived in perfect time – the Bingo Game was over and the barbecue had just begun. The winning raffle number would be announced after the dishing of barbecue chicken and potato salad. Este and June scooted in as quick and quiet as two women ill at ease at church gatherings could scoot, when one of them is nearly ninety.

Taking seats near the door, June leaned into Este and whispered, "Will there be any Mormons here?"

"Nope. Just Lutherans, June."

"Good. I'm scared of Mormons."

Este elbowed June in the ribs like they were two kids in school. "Why? More mens the merrier, June."

"Ssshhh, Este, don't talk like that, we're in church." June giggled like a happy little girl though and Este elbowed her in the ribs again.

"Take it easy, Este …. I got that oldeoporosis bone disease you know …."

"So what's the prize, June? What on earth got you out of the house and back into a church for Pete's sakes?"

Before June could answer, a man stood up and cleared his throat. "Well, I bet a crowd this big didn't just show up for God and barbecued chicken, huh? There's nothing beats a horse race to draw a good crowd."

Este frowned. A horse race? In a church?

"So on your mark, get set, let's get going here and draw the winning ticket. Well, folks … here we go … And the winner is number 88."

June was hunched over, searching frantically through the tickets spread out in her lap. Este spotted the lucky ticket first. "There, June – that one!" She pointed out the winning number.

"Oh my Lord …. Este? I won! All my life all's I ever wanted was a good man and a pony … I had the man … and now I've got the pony …"

Este frowned again. "What on earth are you talking about, June?"

As if on cue, out in front of the church barbecue crowd trotted the tiniest little black horse Este had ever seen in her life. Este watched dumbfounded as her friend stood up and waved the winning ticket so wildly she almost fell over. "Here, over here! That's my number! I won! I won the pony!"

June Day was back among the living.

⸺•⸺

It was horses that brought Hank and Este together and it was horses that threatened to tear them apart. Every few months Hank would announce: "It's high time we sold those horses, Este." Every few months he'd cite his newest reason why, but usually he either gave up trying to convince Este, or forgot to.

Once again Hank was keen on selling the horses. Este's horses. Hoping that the momentum of more than one reason might carry him further, Hank now claimed he had two reasons. He started in on reason number one with a fair amount of confidence. "Molly's leaving shortly for Japan and that new job of hers."

"I know that, Hank. Molly's always off for somewhere or another." Este didn't bother to look up from the videos and DVD's she was sorting through.

It was true. Molly, Hank and Este's youngest child, was always on the go since her divorce from Sam. Usually she didn't go further than a day's drive from them, although once she took a computer programming job in Iceland for six months.

"You might think Iceland's all frozen and white, but it's not, Mom. It's all blue," she called Este to say. "I'm sitting here butt naked in a natural thermal springs hot tub and it's like the air itself is blue … warmest shade of blue you could imagine. Even the snow coming down looks blue. Blue with sparks shooting off all around like tiny crystal bullets."

"Japan's a far stretch from Oregon, Este. Molly's not going to be around to ride with you."

Este did look up at this, which she took as an odd remark. "Molly hasn't gone riding with me since her divorce. She's too busy dating."

It was true, Molly had discovered her newfound freedom, and she was doing her best to lose it all over again. Hank looked out the window. "I swear that bamboo shoots right back up over night to where it was I cut it to the day before," Hank said.

Este kept sorting through her movies and Hank shifted uneasily in his chair, wishing he'd made this a yard-working day. Este usually jumped all over him at the slightest mention that they sell the horses. To Hank's surprise, Este suddenly looked at him and smiled. Encouraged, Hank continued. "Well, maybe Molly doesn't ride with you much these days, but at least I had the comfort of knowing that she could. Or she would if I asked her to."

Este started forward, but caught herself. Molly rode with Este by her own volition, and not because of some father-daughter conspiracy: Este was certain of this much when it came to her daughter.

Hank shifted in his chair again; Este's subtle display of tension had not escaped his notice. "Aren't you even a little tired of those horses? God, I wish you'd at least ride on the beach where someone could spot you if you took a header. You're old enough to know better than to ride out in those woods alone. It's not safe. I'm telling you, Este, you shouldn't be riding out in those woods alone!"

Este snorted but kept all thoughts to herself. No one should be riding out in the woods alone, or anywhere else probably – she knew the wisdom of the buddy system. Still, spectator sports and T.V. was a fact of life and Este was married to a number one fan. If she didn't ride those horses, who would?

Hank rolled his eyes. "Molly's shoving off for a foreign country's one reason to sell them … and hell, I like the idea of a road trip or two each year myself."

Este ignored this change of subject. She knew there was a reason why Hank sometimes stumbled along like this. It was the only way he knew how to find out what was on his own mind. Patience was required, patience as well as restraint.

Taking Este's silence as a positive sign, Hank continued. "Este? I'm ready to do some traveling."

"Me, too."

"Really?"

"Yeah … eventually … but we're not selling the horses, Hank. In fact, we're getting a pony."

Hank nearly backpedaled off the kitchen stool. When the mug of hot coffee he'd been holding sloshed all over the counter and his hands, he swore lightly, but he didn't take his eyes off Este. "We are not getting … a pony … No pony," he repeated. "Damn it, Este, you're too old for a pony!"

"Well, tell that to June Day then. It's her pony. She won it at the church raffle and I told her we'd board him for her."

———

It was babies, small children that broke Este up next.

"Mom? Aunt Emma's getting married again."

Este was taking a walk on the beach with Molly.

Este stopped in her tracks. "My little sister's getting married? Married? Teddy just died seven months ago!"

"I know …. but you know Emma. Life marches on."

Este shook her head. "She could have gotten a pony …"

"What?"

"Nothing."

They walked on in silence. Este stopped again to watch a child playing in the sand. "I miss the twins … when are Cooper Lee and Magnum coming back from their dad's?"

"They'll be back this weekend. I told Sam he could keep them a few days longer, I needed the break. Magnum told me last night on the phone that he was milk toast intolerant. Sam insists on feeding them milk toast and Magnum hates it."

"What about Cooper Lee? Gosh, it feels like they've been gone forever."

"Cooper's learned how to mow the lawn. She told me that no one, not even Magnum, can take away the sweet salty feel of solid work between her hands. Isn't that a hoot? Sounds like the spitting image of someone else I know …." Molly looked pointedly at her mother.

Este said nothing.

"You ok, Mom?"

"Yeah …. Go on, I'll catch up with you."

Molly, who'd grown accustomed to her mother's oddly ritual pauses of late, sighed and continued on down the beach alone to look for sand dollars.

Este arranged herself in the sand a polite distance from a child. The little girl, unaware of anything but the sensation of a sandy shore between her toes, plowed sand under with a tiny toy rake. Next she divided her rows in two, patting the sand into perfect little piles. Rolling back on her heels, she cocked her head sharply right then left, not unlike a lone seagull sitting nearby. Then, her tender face alive with the sudden thought of an idea, she scooped the sand into each of her tiny tennis shoes. Finally, she mounted gull feathers for sails atop the little shoe-boats. The transposed seagull nodded approval, waddle-scooting closer.

Este noted all of this and began to worry. She had a good sense of what was next and, what's more, she knew it would never work.

Smiling, the girl carried one of the shoes into the lapping shallow waves and plopped it out into the water. Without so much as an honest try, the shoe boat pitched sideways and sank out of sight.

The child (bravely blinking back tears it seemed to Este) stared in disbelief.

Este, moved by this tender display of courage, simply lost it.

Molly, several yards away, bent over to pick up the perfect find (this one intact! not a blemish on it! lucky, lucky!), twisted around to see what all the commotion was about. There was her mother, the strongest woman she knew, sobbing on the beach in broad daylight.

"What on earth …" Molly ditched the perfect sand dollar and ran for Este and the terry-clothed toddler.

The child's face went red with alarm and the baby stared not at the lost boat now, but at Este. Then, small legs pumping backwards, she hit the ground backside to the sand and began to cry, too.

The little girl's mother, who had kept vigil from a beach blanket of books and toys, moved quickly to her daughter. But only to shield her from the stranger's emotional shipwreck. The seagull squawked off into the sky.

"Mother, what on earth has gotten into you?" Molly asked. "You're scaring people – you're scaring babies." Hugging her mother to her side, she walked Este away and up the beach.

Este wouldn't be consoled. "Tender Littles is what they are," she said. "Hardly out of the can. All these kids, they don't have a clue to what they're up against on this earth. None of us does."

Molly about faced her mother and held her out at arm's length. "What's going on really? Just tell me: what is it?"

"I never was much good to you as a mother, was I?"

Molly's eyes widened. She lifted her mother's chin, forcing Este to look at her. "You were wonderful … you are wonderful. Don't doubt yourself like this! Stop it."

Este's shoulders hunched, began to shake; Molly pulled her mother into her arms. "It's all right – everything will be all right. You understand that?"

No. Este didn't. But she nodded her head anyway.

———

"Lizbeth tells me I'm trying to take her identity. No, take on her identity … she told me that. She says I've been doing it to her all her life. How on earth do you take on someone else's identity, Este?"

It was Emma. Emma had these strained moments (emotional sparring events really), that bordered on the physical between herself and her only child, Lizbeth.

"… way Lizbeth tells it, I stole her childhood. Tells me she was more my mother that I ever was hers. What kind of thing is that for a kid to say to her own mother? Can you believe it?"

For the most part Este could believe it. It was that middle sibling thing. Emma, sandwiched between an older sister and a younger brother all her life, believed herself to be the invisible child.

Este almost sympathized with Lizbeth. Emma seemed to need an inordinate amount of mothering. But it was never enough. It was like someone standing around handing someone else money. At what point would the person receiving the money walk away?

"What did you say back to her?" Este asked, though she was pretty certain this was the wrong question to ask. But the mindless comforting sounds of a surrogate mother who was, after all, just an older sister, could only go so far.

"I didn't … couldn't say anything … I was speechless! So I cried. And then she hung up on me, just like that. My own daughter hung up on me!"

Good for Lizbeth. It had often been Este's suspicion that a good slap upside the head by one to the other – either Lizbeth or Emma, it didn't much matter who initiated it – might result in the necessary shock, and thus peace, each was longing to find. Lizbeth's hanging up on Emma seemed a firm step in that direction.

"Well, that's too bad. Must be hard on both of you."

"I wish I had the relationship you and Molly have."

"What makes you think our relationship's any different?" It was different, but that wasn't what Emma wanted to hear.

"It just is – I'm a great observer of things like that."

Emma made the sniffing sound that Este had come to associate with her sister's feeling more pleased with herself than she let on. "Jim called last night." Emma sniffed again.

"A-ha," said Este.

"What's that supposed to mean?" Emma asked suspiciously.

"Nothing."

Which was an out and out lie; nevertheless it gave Este a warm feeling of satisfaction that she'd been correct in sensing Emma's true motive for calling.

"We're getting together to decide what it is we should do about Lizbeth, after you know what."

Without waiting for a reply from Este, Emma prattled on about a salesman who'd just sold her a three month supply of vitamins and herbal extracts guaranteed to boost her female hormones to normal levels again. "You might want to give them a try, Este, seeing as how you're older than I am."

"What does Lizbeth have to say about all that?"

"Hormones? She's too young for hormones to give her any grief. Oh … You meant what does Lizbeth have to say about Jim? Lord, Este, sometimes I wonder where your mind's at. I – that is, we – haven't told her yet."

"You haven't told her."

"We need to tell her together. Of course I haven't told her, that's my point."

But of course. Emma needed a good audience almost more than she needed mothering. Why on earth did Este keep thinking anyone – much less anyone related by blood to her – would do things different from how they'd done them all their lives?

Este took a deep breath and blew it back out to the count of ten. But instead of her perturbation subsiding, she felt her body go cold and burn with fire at the same time. Then, like a nagging spouse, a particular thought broke through the clouds of her personal weather. Lord, what a bother – such a memory she had. There was that word again. Pause. According to the stress reduction tapes, she was to step out of her life at times like this. Die on purpose, they called it. Forget the heave ho, fight 'em and right 'em, and instead, take a break: pause. Breathe, even.

Why then, did the image of Mel Gibson on a jigging horse insist on showing up in her mind?

Este did her best to keep her mouth shut, did her best not to speak her mind till she could speak it to herself, alone. Or maybe to Hank in semi-private, when he was confronted by the evening news, and less inclined to impart his point of view on the matter.

But sometimes best wasn't that so much as it was being prudent. And Este, prudent by nature, birth order, and one too many English forebears, had come to appreciate her Scottish ancestry more. Thanks to Mel Gibson – who also rode in on a black horse whenever he needed the shield and furor of candor.

"What's your point, Emma?"

Or that was what Este thought she'd said. What she really said was something else. What she really said – such a memory, hers – were the lines from Dr. Zhivago: "Your point. Her village."

Emma was silent, though only briefly. "Este, you're making less and less sense these days. But to answer your question, my point is Lizbeth should respect her elders. She's about to have two of them again."

Este exhaled her die on purpose breath in a splutter of spit and air. Well, she had managed a pregnant pause anyway. The stress reduction experts would have to grant her that much.

"Why the hell would she do that, Emma? As your daughter has so perfectly pointed out, Lizbeth's more your elder than you are hers. You act more like her spoiled kid sister than an elder. And a snob to boot."

Though a line from Ryan's Daughter put it best. Unfortunately, Este's memory had its limits. So she was only able to recall the line in hindsight after Emma hung up on her.

Of course she's a snob. Wasn't that what the English were famous for?

Hank had quit riding a few years earlier. He told Este that he had lost interest in horses and riding altogether, but Este knew it had more to do with the last spill he'd taken off of his mare, Babe. Hank and Este had been on one of their all day rides, and Babe, refusing to cross a creek, let Hank cross it without her. Hank began his journey across the creek head first, but he was able to twist himself in the air in such a way that initially it looked like he might land on his feet. Este kept her fingers crossed and tried not to wince as her husband flew through the air.

Hank didn't land on his feet. He landed, like a shamed ice skater, hard on his ass. The water made his landing a little easier – his aging bones crashed into the shallow, rocky creek bed – but not much. Now whenever Hank overdoes it with yard-work, his lower back where he hit the ground gives him trouble.

At the time the doctor had said it was his coccyx, but Este thought the doctor had said something else. Hank vowed never to set foot in a doctor's office again after Este endorsed out loud in front of strangers, her agreement with what she thought had been the physician's diagnosis.

Despite Hank's embarrassment, Este wasn't way off the mark. For age has a way of rendering soft those things that should go hard, just as it can harden up those things that should say soft – like kind words for a sick animal or a frightened child. It was her observation that if you don't pay attention, age can cause a person to become unlike anyone or anything you ever imagined they might be. And sometimes it will do that even if you do pay attention.

"Damn horses … damn that old mare," Hank says if ever he thinks Este's not close enough to hear him. Why do the kids feel the need to live so far away? Iceland? Brazil? God damn it, the whole world's gone nuts. What the hell's it all about anyway?"

Este didn't know why this was, but Hank often felt the need to ride his worldly concerns right up alongside his resentment of the mare who had brought him and Este together. Once while nailing up a sheet of drywall, he realized Este had heard him cussing Babe out loud. Hank blushed and fumbled with his hammer, dropping it to the ground. He turned away, as if ashamed.

Instead of letting things take their own course, Este made the mistake of trying to lighten things up again. "Really now, Hank: stop riding that dead horse. Stop, already."

Hank slowly turned towards Este. For a split second she had the awful thought that he might hit her, though Hank had never been a violent man. It was like he'd forgotten where he was, or even who he was, but only for a moment. Then he held his arms out wide for Este and when she walked inside them, she felt his whole body tremble.

"Don't talk like that, Este," he said in between catching his breath. "Don't ever let me hear you say such a thing again."

Age not only has a way of catching up on you, it can leave you far behind. Or far ahead, or whatever it is that happens when the act of growing old doesn't present a problem any more. Case in point? Babe. A little off her feed one night, Este failed to pay attention to the signs of a belly ache gone south real quick. Old Babe colicked that night and died. Imagining that her tender old guts twisted till they burst inside, Este's own stomach hurt for days. It grieved her no end that this creature who had served them faithfully for years had died in the dark of night, alone, and probably in pain.

"There was nothing you could have done, honey," Hank had told her. "She was old. There was absolutely nothing you could have done. These things happen."

These things may happen, but it never gets any easier, the losing of these things that matter. Lord knows Este had lost more than her share of good animals. The only consolation she had about Babe was that she had twenty-three years behind her. That was pretty old for a horse.

But in Este's forever reflecting mind, Heidi had twenty-three years behind her also. And that was nothing like old! Oh, hell no: that was prime time for a woman to be walking down the middle of town in a wet suit with stray dogs nipping at her ankles. Prime time. Este took a deep breath and blew it back out again. She smiled. So what then, if it was outrageous? Flamboyant besides? In the overall scheme of things, what real harm then?

After all, it too would pass.

Este paddled out on her board well past where she knew the first set of waves would roll in, determined to stay on this side of trouble. It was her first time in the ocean in three years. Three years since she'd last surfed, three years since she'd been out on the ocean and a board again. The simple physical act of paddling was adrenaline enough to sign her up for happy again – she hadn't even caught a wave yet.

Hank had made her an appointment with a doctor. A head doctor, a shrink. He thought Este was losing her mind. Well, he hadn't said as much but there it was: Este had an appointment the following day with a stranger, a man, a person who sat you down in a room (or did they lay you out on a couch?) where you were supposed to talk about what was going on inside of you. But Este was never very good at talking, her words had a way of coming out ahead of her own thinking, especially with a stranger asking questions that she considered no one's business but her own.

Este straddled her board like it was a horse, legs dangling in the water. Shark bait, Hank had teased her. Shark bait. Well, none of us are going to get out of here alive, Hank. And on that note, Este shoved herself forward on her belly again and paddled fierce and strong as the first set of waves rolled in.

Taking off on a gentle swell that lifted her up light and happy as only a wave can do, Este stood on her board and raced towards the shore.

"So … what is it brought you here to see me today?" asked the psychologist.

Este had kept her appointment. Well, she had made plans to skip out and go surfing instead, but Hank literally put a stop to that. He'd been watching from the living-room window and as soon as he saw her come out of the garage with her board in tow, he opened up a window and yelled. "Stop right there. This is not a game, Este, and you are not in high school."

"Tide's just right, Hank – it's two hours coming in still!"

"Tide comes in twice a day, Este. Always has, always will. You can catch the next one. You're keeping this appointment, Este. It means something to me."

"My husband made this appointment, I'm just keeping it for him."

Lance chuckled.

"Why's that funny?"

"I'm sorry, it was my first reaction is all. I've never had someone come in here by way of an appointment made by a spouse before. It's not how I like to do things but I made an exception in your case."

"Why? Do you know my husband – you a friend or something?"

"No, not exactly. But he did put out a small fire at my place once."

Este smiled, shook her head.

"What? What crossed your mind just then?"

Este sat up straighter in her seat. The man really was a head doctor. Well, she'd see just how good he was at reading between the lines then.

"Oh … my husband's pretty good at putting out fires."

Lance shoved back in his chair, clapped his hands together and positively grinned. Before Este could resist, she grinned back.

"Bingo. School's out, kid … first session's over. But I need you to do some home-work …"

---

It didn't present a problem at first. Hank thought it kind of cute, really. He watched as Este pretended to reorganize the cupboards in the kitchen, glancing back to his newspaper just in time when Este darted a look his way before sneaking a favorite coffee mug or soup bowl into the wooden crate she kept hidden beneath the kitchen sink. The crate contained her tree-house stash. It had already made several trips out to the front yard and back to the house again. Hank was careful to study its contents from time to time, seriously contemplating interference on his end when what was in the box threatened to fall into the category of fire hazard.

When Este scooted out to the post office each day, Hank pulled out the crate and methodically went through each and every one of its contents, hesitating over an ancient box of fireplace matches and several old burned down candles. He reluctantly placed these things back in the crate only after he'd weighed all possibilities in his mind. Este was after all, a grown woman. She had raised their two children with both his and the community's approval, even applause for the individual aplomb she'd brought to the job. Este was greatly responsible also for navigating Hank and their crew towards this quieter passage in their lives, this sudden shore beside calmer waters. She was as solid, still, as the foundation of their home – wasn't she?

What small matter was this then, a grown woman with a tree house?

Este scrunched down low on the floor of her tree house, trying to stay invisible to anyone driving up and down the road beside their driveway. Coast was clear. Standing back up, she uncoiled an eighty foot orange extension cord. Next she built a single large loop. Then, taking aim like she might have off her horse when setting out to rope an imaginary cow for imaginary doctoring, Este tossed her loop straight into the air where it fell back against the house and a single outside electrical outlet. Scrambling down from the tree house (after checking that the coast was still clear), Este plugged in the end of her long orange rope and climbed back up into the tree house.

Este moved cautiously across the floor on her hands and knees to a small braided rug where she'd set a small TV with a built-in DVD player. Then slowly, with all the luxury of a child (she thought of baby Molly once upon a time up high on her toes, moving in a daze towards the idiot box and Captain Kangaroo), Este sprawled spread-eagled on her belly, and began to do her homework.

"You got her doing what?"

"Watching old movies."

"Hells bells, I told you Este already does that."

"Well, Hank, sometimes the best way to put out a fire is to fan the flames even more."

Hank looked doubtful. He also hoped the psychotherapist never asked to be a volunteer at his fire department. "Well ...." Hank's voice trailed off; he shrugged in resignation.

"Don't worry so much," said Lance. "We're moving in a particular direction here ...."

Backwards maybe? Or just sideways off a cliff altogether? Or hell! Who needed a cliff? Este had a tree house she could tumble out of just fine. Hank kept these thoughts to himself though. "Ok ... I'll go along .... Guess I need to trust your judgment here."

"Really? Just like that?"

"You're the doctor."

"Ok, then. Well, trust this: you need to make an appointment with me too."

Holy shit. Hank never saw the trailer to that movie.

---

Hank vowed never to set foot in a head doctor's office ever again. My Lord, what was it gave a doctor over to thinking they were God? Hank found himself talking about things he'd made a point of never thinking about again! Things he never knew he felt so strongly about, like the little dog he used to have. Hank took the dog everywhere he went. Back when Hank still smoked and it was time to go outside for a walk and a Malboro Light, the little dog would light out like a tiny flame itself at the flick of Hank's lighter.

Years later, after the dog had died, and after Hank had quit smoking, he kept the lighter in the chest pocket of his shirt. In part for the sweet smoky sadness of cigarette nostalgia, and in part for memory of the dog.

He still missed that dog something fierce.

Damn that shrink for bringing it all back up! They didn't call it a flood of memories for nothing. And as for the indirect suggestion that Hank leave Este, even for a short separation, no, no, no. Never. Hank saw what happened to those men .... the lonely figure of his old friend Abe shuffling down the street in some bizarre attempt at taking up jogging for the first time in fifty years.

No, no, a thousand times no.

—————

Este was sick and tired of these people. Screw the new California friends and clients with La Jolla horse ranches and Oregon beach houses. So what if they made little chocolate porpoises, donating ten percent to dolphins everywhere? She'd like to hear one dolphin's opinion on that. What the hell did a dolphin do with ten percent anyway?

For that matter, screw the old friends from California too. Especially old friends like her brother-in-law Teddy who waxed on and on in some Zen Buddhist New-Age-mangled version of teaching a man to fish instead of just giving him one. Heck, the way Este figured it, if a man was truly hungry he'd be hard put to go out and fish up a fish in the cold dark wet of Oregon, for Pete's sakes.

She had especially disliked the way Teddy started all his sentences with "karmatically speaking …."

While driving Teddy through downtown Portland, Este saw a father and his young daughter pushing a grocery store basket down the street with what looked like their life's belongings. "What about that child?" asked Este. "She's not old enough to have karma, Teddy. She's not old enough to have a learner's permit for karma. What about her, Teddy?"

Este may have grown up on a farm, but she hadn't completely missed the sixties, thank-you much. When was it that the teachings of Christ or Buddha had become only mantric pathways to clarity and efficiency in the work place? What happened to plain-fashioned compassion for what stood smack in front of you?

What kind of god was that? Jesus Christ indeed!

"I see what your concern is, Este, but reframe it. They're building character in this life for the next one. It's not tragic, it's where they're at. Suffering is a part of life and it's kind of exciting, really, if you see it as one more experience on an individual's path. It's best not to interfere with it. Not even when it seems insufferable to us."

Este had turned to look at Teddy in disbelief, nearly running into the car in front of them. She pulled off to the side of the road in midday traffic and stopped the car, looked long and hard at Teddy, scratched the back of her neck and did what the stress reduction expert on the tape had told her to do.

Este paused in her life. She stopped right then and there, if only to make certain she was clear that her next action might wreak irrevocable havoc on her life – or this particular friendship anyway.

"I'd like you to get out of my car, Teddy. Too much suffering never put up a Starbucks, I know that much. You can trust your own experience to find your way home again. Your karma hath run over my dogma, friend."

---

"Was that absolutely necessary?" said Lance. Este had just related the story to him in one of their sessions.

"Thanks a lot! Teddy's dead. I already feel terrible."

"Well, learn from it then, damn it. Don't feel terrible. That's a cop-out."

Este, thoroughly startled, pushed back in her chair and said with as much dignity as she could muster, "I believe I was doing the best I could at the time."

"I thought you said you never had therapy before."

"I haven't."

"That's the classic cop-out line delivered by therapists all over the country. I should know, I've cast that line into a few troubled waters myself."

Este was quiet; Lance continued.

"Don't you think you were experiencing a kind of collective angst perhaps? A frustration for the world's problems maybe? Which none of us really has an answer for, so was that really fair to put all of that on Teddy?"

Este snorted. "Yeah. At the time I thought it was."

"Meaning?"

"Meaning …. Meaning it was probably his kaaaaaarma."

Lance put his face down in his hands and said nothing.

Este pushed herself back in her chair in retreat of Lance's disapproval. Resisting all inclination to steal a look at him, she scowled at the floor instead. Here she was alive and kicking and Teddy was dead. But Este still stood by her point of view. At least she stood by something, which was more than she could say about her brother-in-law. Overthrow what Teddy called Clinton's Democratic Kingdom indeed. Hell! Fifty thousand roping lessons later, Teddy still never could hit a dummy at two feet away and a standstill. There was no overthrowing monarchies where that came from.

Lance finally looked up again. "You have two problems I see right now. One is you're too short. I can't do anything about that."

"What's my other problem?" Este wasn't concerned about her height and figured Lance was kidding besides. She'd known men all her life who stood eye to eye with even the biggest and tallest of horses, but sometimes that caused more problems than it solved.

"You tell me."

"I thought that's what my husband hired you to do: tell me."

"Ok, time's up."

Este knew when a point of departure was being offered. She rose to her feet, launching up onto the toes of her boots briefly. She gave Lance a grim smile. "Seems I'm a disappointment … one of the nuts you failed to crack. Maybe … maybe I don't want to be cracked. I vote this be our last session – nothing personal, I just need to figure things out on my own's all."

Lance, too startled to show it, simply nodded. He mumbled something to Este's back as she turned away and then watched as Este prepared to leave his office, prepared to take with her the unfathomable, willful moods she seemed to stir up in others by virtue of her simple presence.

"Stay in your own movie, ok, Este?"

Este gave Lance a questioning look. "What?"

"Ken Kesey – oh … never mind."

As if Lance had never spoken, Este walked through the door without so much as a word of thanks, or even, goodbye.

Este had had it; she wasn't taking any more crap from the likes of anyone. Her mood being what it was, Este wasn't taking any more crap from June Day's pony either. Each day when she went to put the tiny horse out with the others, the mini monster mare spun off like the proverbial bat out of hell. It was rude and crude behavior for a member of Este's horse herd, pure and simple. It suggested, also, a lack of control on the horse handler's part. Este cared even less for this suggestion.

When next she went to put the tiny mare out with the others, Este took along her rope. Tossing a loop about the little horse's head, she left it dangling down upon the pony's shoulders. Although she couldn't see its eyes beneath the tangled matt of forelock that made the pony look like a Bangladesh street urchin, she knew the pony was watching her. Intensely. Este stared right back where she imagined its eyes to be, till the pony, decidedly unperturbed, put her head down to graze.

"Food for thought, is it pony? Well, chew on it and every right thought you get from that, then."

Some overwhelming sense that the pony didn't have shit for brains occurred to Este – or that the pony thought this about her. This last thought was irksome to say the least. Este felt the familiar rise in adrenalin, the hot rush of anger that followed closely on such heels and … she took a deep breath and blew it back out again. Anger didn't work, such a state usually got the best of her – especially when it came to horses. Maybe the pony did have shit for brains, but today's natural horsemanship principles did not include voicing such ideas out loud.

Este had made such a mistake with June – she had voiced aloud her opinion that maybe, probably, the pony was bothered beyond repair. There was an old saying: "Never look a gift horse in the mouth." Well, scratch that when it came to winning lottery tickets that got you a pony. It didn't take but a couple of days for Este to figure out why the pony had shown up in a church raffle. Only Jesus could love such a beast. Jesus, and June Day.

For the pony was June's newfound religion. Each day June showed up with offerings of carrots and apples. Each day the pony did its best to take a bite, land a kick, or rush with ears pinned towards the bewildered old woman who had near the love of Jesus to give to that little mare. No matter what the pony dished out, June was born again, determined to stay a believer.

Este on the other hand, was more an agnostic when it came to the tiny hoofed devil. Her roping days weren't over yet.

Este next dallied tight the other end of the rope to a piling off the deck of the house, figuring the post solid enough to have leashed and kept afloat the sinking Titantic.

Este hadn't figured on Titantic II.

Carefully undoing the halter, she quietly lifted it away from the horse's face, one hand cradling the tiny mare's silky nose in a suggestion to stay put till Este formally released her. Suggestion notwithstanding, the pony mare, the second she felt the halter in the air and not on her face, lunged for freedom. Este simply stepped aside, and waited.

"Cowboy up, pony. I dare you to sink that."

The mare made a beeline for the other horses, quick as spit – and hit the end of the rope. Surprised, the pony braced itself for a brief moment and lunged forward again, this time flipping up and over, landing right side up like Tanya Harding before Nancy Kerrigan's knee ruined all chances for glory. A bit shaken, the pony collapsed to the ground, but she quickly scrambled up again, bolting to the right this time.

Este, cocky as the Sundance Kid up to this point, knew she was losing ground. What's more, self-respect. The pony didn't hit the end of the rope with a wild whoa like horses were supposed to do. This pony didn't do anything like horses were supposed to do. What the heck was wrong with this po ---- neeee -- "

Before Este could complete the thought, something hit her from behind, knocking Este out from under Este. All thoughts past, present and future, disappeared from her mind.

Este was out stone cold.

⸺

When she came to, Hank was holding her in his arms. "Este? I need you to say something. Talk to me … what's your name?"

Este moaned and hid her face in Hank's shirt.

"How many fingers am I holding before you, Este? Tell me ... how many – "

"I don't want to count your fingers, Hank – and you already know my name. I want to stay like this for awhile. Hold me ... just hold me."

———

"911, 911 we have an emergency: two children missing, two children and, er, uh, a pony? Yes, that's right, two children and a pony – no, no, I don't mean a large dog, I mean a pony. A real pony. Let's focus here, the two children are priority over the pony but the kids went looking for the lost pony, and now they're lost, too. To heck with the pony, we gotta' find those kids. Come again? Six years old, both of them. They're twins, a girl and a boy. Fire Chief McCall's grandchildren to be precise. This is an emergency: Chief McCall's grand-babies are missing."

———

They found the pony and the children a few hundred yards from the tree house in the adjoining woods by the McCall's home. It was an unremark-able search, but a very remarkable find. The pony was lying quietly in a small clearing, Cooper Lee and Magnum flanking her sides. The rope was gone from her neck. In the rope's place were Cooper Lee's and Magnum's tee shirts tied together and knotted about the pony's head in a makeshift halter. They'd used a piece of baling twine for a lead rope.

"She's tired," said Cooper Lee.

"She's hungry," said Magnum.

"She likes Frosted Mini wheats," added Cooper. "Like me."

"And me," said Magnum.

Sure enough, the pony was eating cereal from a plastic container.

Este walked quietly up to the pony and held out her hand. The pony smelled it agreeably enough, her warm breath almost an apology. For the briefest of moments the pony looked full on into Este's eyes then went back to eating her cereal. Este sank to the ground and her grandchildren. Like a beautiful, slightly sad little song, the kids wailed: "We don't want to go to Japan, G'andma. We want to stay here with you and G'andpa and June Day's pony."

If wishes were ponies, we'd all be riding thought Este. Well hell, let's go riding then.

---

"So what was it brought you out of your tree-house to see me again, Este?" asked Lance.

"That this was all I had left if I were to lose my husband. That this was what it had come to if Hank were to die …. There I was, sitting up in a tree and I realized all I'd become was a woman past middle age with a tree house and a spoiled pony. All the years of horse work and babies with my man (a kind of glory wasn't it?), all of that had become more like a story about someone else's life than it was my own … and I couldn't feel it any more. It was like it was all a moving picture show … like one of those movies I watch over and over again except I can feel the movies. I just couldn't feel my own life any more."

"And?" said Lance.

Because he knew there was an "and" to all of this. Not because he thought he was God. Not even. A colleague once told Lance that Lance attracted the kind of clients he did out of a sense of superiority, that his clients very lack of status in the world was a direct reflection of Lance's superiority complex.

But Lance knew this to be all terribly wrong. If anything, he felt inferior. Because Este, what with all her restlessness and "temporary out of sortness" (her words actually), fit her life.

Lance did not fit his life.

"So the thought I had up in my tree house was this one: somehow, all along, even when I was a little kid, it was in me to have a life like this. An aging woman with a tree house and a pony I didn't trust to take a monkey for a ride. Then along comes these two children, my own flesh and blood … and the two of them tame this pony in an instant. They tame him like magic. And boy oh boy, did I ever feel that. This is my life, Dr. Lance. This is my crazy freakin' life and … and I love it. I wasn't sure any longer but I am now. I … love … my … life."

Lance alternately clasped his hands together and fluttered them out to his sides. He pressed the toes of his shoes into the floor, then lifted his heels as if to take flight and plant himself solid at the same time. He looked like a very tired eagle trying to see his way clear for a landing.

The weary eagle leaned forward in his chair and made as if to say something to Este; he doubled over at the waist as if in pain. Lance didn't look at Este. He couldn't look at Este. Instead he stared off across the room, his fists stacked one atop the other in front of his chest, one potato, two potato. The wings of a great bird turned back into the hands of a man who thought too much. He shifted in his seat, restacked his fists. Three potato, four. Wiggled his thumbs in the air – thumpkin, thumbkin, where was Thumbkin? Took a deep breath, released it slowly: one, two, three, four. Five potato, more.

Finally, finally, he looked at Este. Bravely, bravely, Lance smiled. And when he stood and held his arms wide, Este was there to receive what his complicated body language had already expressed, and as she walked inside the strangely comforting cave of his arms, Este felt Lance's whole body relax.

Lance Dubois had come unfisted.

Breinigsville, PA USA
30 December 2010
252458BV00001B/2/P